Sylvie counted silent~~ly~~ ~~under her~~ breath. "*When* do you want to work ~~on the~~ project, Carlos?"

Carlos shrugged. "I'll call you. Okay?"

"No, it is *not* okay!" Sylvie yelled. She didn't care if every kid in the schoolyard heard her. "McCracken is going to kill us if we don't do a good job. And tomorrow night is Parents' Night!"

Desdemona stepped in front of Sylvie. "I thought you were Sylvie's best friend," she said to Carlos.

"Ortega doesn't hang with girls," Michael said. He put an arm around Carlos's shoulders. "Besides, we guys have plans."

"Your plans are bad news," Desdemona told him.

Sylvie tried again. "Carlos," she said.

Michael started to laugh. "She's so dense," he said to Carlos. "She just doesn't get it."

"Get what?" Sylvie demanded.

"Even a first-grader would get the message," Michael said. "Tell her, Ortega!"

Carlos looked at the ground. "Get lost, Sylvie. *Just get lost!*"

Meet all the kids in McCracken's Class:

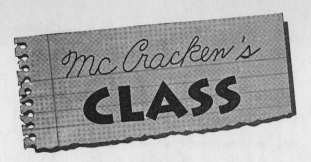

#1

GET LOST, SYLVIE!

by Diana Oliver

BULLSEYE BOOKS
Random House 🏠 New York

For Phyllis Steiber and Barbara Steiber—
the best of sisters, the best of friends—
and with thanks to Lisa Banim
for all the good ideas

A BULLSEYE BOOK PUBLISHED BY RANDOM HOUSE

Copyright © 1993 by Random House, Inc.
Cover design by Michaelis/Carpelis Design Associates, Inc.
Cover art copyright © 1993 by Melodye Rosales. All rights reserved
under International and Pan-American Copyright Conventions.
Published in the United States by Random House, Inc.,
and simultaneously in Canada
by Random House of Canada Limited, Toronto.
Library of Congress Catalog Card Number: 93-83962
ISBN: 0-679-84988-2
RL: 4.1

Manufactured in the United States of America
10 9 8 7 6 5 4 3 2 1

MCCRACKEN'S CLASS is a trademark of Random House, Inc.

"Sylvie, Sylvie!"

Sylvie Levine stuck the knife back in the peanut butter jar and turned around. Her little sister, Willa, was clutching her leg.

"What's up, Willa?" Sylvie asked.

"Take me to fif grade," Willa said.

"Fif*th*," Sylvie said, bending down to give her sister a hug. "And I'm real sorry, but I can't take you to school with me."

"Why not?" Willa asked.

"Because they don't allow three-year-olds in the fifth grade," Sylvie explained patiently.

Mrs. Levine walked into the kitchen, running a hand through her short, dark hair. She and Willa looked a lot alike, but Sylvie had long, wavy red hair and blue eyes.

"'Morning, sweetie," Mrs. Levine said, dropping a kiss on the top of Sylvie's head. She squinted up at the clock on the kitchen wall. "It's only seven o'clock. What are you doing up so early?"

"I was too excited to sleep," Sylvie said.

Her mother began to make coffee. "I used to be excited about the first day of school, too," she said. "I always wore my best dress." She glanced back at Sylvie and frowned. "Honey, is that what you're wearing?"

"Yep." Sylvie had chosen her striped polo shirt, jeans, and purple high-tops very carefully. "Carlos and I are going to play soccer after school." Carlos Ortega was Sylvie's best friend. His family had lived across the street for as long as Sylvie could remember.

Her mother sighed and poured a glass of juice for Willa. "What did you eat for breakfast?"

"Cereal," Sylvie said. "And toast and orange juice. I just finished making my lunch. And last night I put my pens and pencils in my pack."

Mrs. Levine set Willa on a chair and sat down at the table. "Sounds like you've got just about everything. Your dad left you something on the couch."

Sylvie's eyes lit up. Mr. Levine sometimes went on trips to buy things for her parents' antique store, Past Times. This week he was in Maine. Sylvie always missed her dad when

2

he was away, but it was great when he left her presents.

She ran into the living room. There on the big red velvet couch was a package wrapped in gold paper. She quickly tore it open and found a three-ring notebook. Its cover was made of soft, faded blue leather, exactly the color of the sky before a thunderstorm. On the inside, Mr. Levine had written:

> *For Sylvie on her first day of*
> *fifth grade. Hope you have a*
> *great year!*
>
> *Love, Dad*

Sylvie ran her hand over the leather cover. No one in her class would have a notebook like this. It wasn't the kind of notebook you could buy in the neighborhood stationery store. Sylvie liked to write stories, and she knew she'd write great ones in this notebook.

She checked her watch. Carlos would be coming in five minutes so they could walk to school together.

She took her denim jacket from the hallway closet. "I'm going," she called.

Mrs. Levine came into the hall. "I want you home by five," she said.

"No problem," Sylvie said. The doorbell

rang just as she was stuffing her new notebook in her pack.

"That's Carlos," she said. "I'm out of here."

The sky was a clear blue and the fall air was cool. Sylvie buttoned her denim jacket as she stepped out onto the porch of her building. "Hey, Carlos," she said.

"Hey, Sylvie," Carlos replied. Carlos was skinny and taller than Sylvie. He had curly black hair and wire-rimmed glasses. He was wearing a long-sleeved T-shirt, jeans, and high-tops. Today he wasn't carrying a pack or even a notebook. He just had a lunch bag in his hand and a pen sticking out of his back pocket.

"I can't believe summer's over," Carlos said as they started down Elm Street. "Goodbye freedom."

"I know," Sylvie said with a sigh. "But at least we're in the same class again." She and Carlos had already compared room numbers.

Carlos shrugged. "I just hope we get Ms. Rivers."

"Didn't Roberto have McCracken?" Sylvie asked. Roberto was Carlos's older brother.

"He sure did," Carlos said. "He even has a T-shirt that says, 'I survived McCracken's class.'"

"He does not," Sylvie said.

"Yeah, he does. He just never wears it to school."

"Your sister told me McCracken's hair's got so much hair spray in it, it never moves," Sylvie said. "All the girls call her Helmet Hair." She shuddered. "I *definitely* want Ms. Rivers."

"McCracken gave Roberto fourteen detentions," Carlos said.

"Fourteen?" Sylvie gasped.

Carlos shrugged. "Roberto gets good grades, but he can be a real pain. I wouldn't want to be his teacher."

They passed Chang's Chinese Restaurant and Luigi's Pizza Parlor. Big old oak and chestnut trees lined Grant Avenue, where the Music Corner and the stationery store and Ice Cream Heaven were. Best of all, Newton's Newsstand was on Grant.

Sylvie stopped as they reached the newsstand. "Hi, Newton!" she called to the tall Jamaican man behind the counter.

"Good morning, Sylvie. 'Morning, Carlos," Newton said. "What are you two doing, bothering me so early?" he asked with a wink.

"It's the first day of school," Sylvie said.

"So what grade are you in now?" Newton said, stroking his chin. "Third?" He chuckled

5

at the indignant looks Sylvie and Carlos gave him. "All right, all right," he said. "I know you're in fifth. But let me give you a little piece of advice. You'd better mind your step around that Ms. McCracken."

"You had her too?" Sylvie asked.

Newton laughed his deep laugh. "Ms. McCracken isn't that old, child. But my oldest boy, Winston, was in her class. The kids called her 'Crack-the-Whip McCracken.'"

Sylvie bit her lip. "We're hoping we get Ms. Rivers."

"Well, good luck," Newton said. "Otherwise, you two, watch yourselves." He handed Sylvie and Carlos each a gumball wrapped in plastic. "Here you go. For the first day of school, they're on me. Just don't you be chewing them in the classroom."

"We won't," Sylvie promised. "Thanks, Newton."

"Later," Carlos told Newton.

"Later yourself," Newton replied.

Sylvie and Carlos continued walking down Grant until they reached Harry Park. And at the very edge of Harry Park was Martin Luther King, Jr., Elementary.

Sylvie's heart began to beat faster as she neared the familiar red-brick building. She hated feeling this nervous.

"Yo, Levine!" A tall, tough-looking girl with brown hair and a scar on her lip stepped in front of Sylvie.

Sylvie stepped back. Ronnie Smith was her least favorite person in the whole world. Ronnie loved to pick fights. Even the sixth-graders were afraid of her. And she had a gang of three other girls who were every bit as mean as she was.

"Hi, Ronnie," Sylvie said without enthusiasm. She looked around the schoolyard, but she didn't see Ronnie's sidekicks anywhere. At least Carlos was there beside her.

"Listen, wuss," Ronnie said. "I thought I told you not to come back to school this year." Ronnie leaned close to Sylvie's face. "You should have paid attention, Levine. I'm gonna make you sorry you ever showed up."

"We're just sorry we have to look at you," Carlos told her.

"You're on my list, too, Ortega," Ronnie promised. Then she turned and stomped off, probably to go pick on someone else.

"You shouldn't have said that," Sylvie said when Ronnie was gone.

"Don't worry about it," Carlos said. "What's she going to do?"

"Beat me up!" Sylvie said. Ronnie was always threatening to beat her up.

"She won't touch you," Carlos said. "I won't let her."

That made Sylvie feel a little better, but it didn't make her feel safe. Ronnie was a lot bigger than Carlos.

Just then, the first bell rang and the huge green doors to the school opened. "Let's go," Carlos said.

Sylvie and Carlos went into the school. The halls smelled of fresh floor polish and chalk dust. It was a smell Sylvie loved.

"Where are we supposed to go again?" Carlos checked the card in his pocket. "Room 206."

He and Sylvie walked up the stairs to the second floor, then down a long hall to a corner classroom.

Sylvie peered inside Room 206 and quickly shrank back. "Oh, no," she said.

"What's wrong?"

"Ronnie Smith is in there," Sylvie said with a gulp.

"Big deal," Carlos said.

"That's not all," Sylvie said. "So is Ms. McCracken!"

Sylvie stood outside the classroom door as the other kids streamed inside. She didn't move.

"Sylvie," Carlos said, "let's go."

"I'm not going in there," Sylvie said.

"You have to," Carlos said. "This is school, remember?"

Sylvie crossed her arms and shook her head. "McCracken's class *and* Ronnie Smith? No way. I'm going to get my parents to transfer me to Ms. Rivers's class."

"Right now?" Carlos asked.

Sylvie looked at her watch. At the moment her father was in Maine, and her mother was opening the shop. "Probably not right now," she admitted.

"Is there a problem here?"

Sylvie's heart sank as she looked up to see a tall woman staring down at them. The woman had a long, sharp nose and poufy orange hair. Sylvie looked closely at the hair. Sure enough, it was teased up to look full, and then sprayed in place. Definitely Helmet Hair.

"What are your names?" Ms. McCracken demanded.

"Sylvie Levine," Sylvie said.

"Carlos Ortega," Carlos added.

"Well, you're both in my class," Ms. McCracken said. "I suggest you march yourselves inside before the late bell rings. I do not tolerate lateness in my class."

Sylvie stepped into the classroom, feeling sick. Fifth grade was not going to be great, or even okay. Fifth grade was going to be a disaster.

Sylvie looked around as Ms. McCracken took attendance. Besides Ronnie Smith, there were some okay kids in her class, especially Annie Tuzmarti. Secretly, Sylvie had always wanted to be friends with Annie, but Annie had loads of friends already. John Jerome was cute, even though he liked to tease girls. Rosa Santiago, who always got straight A's, sat near the front of the class. Jimmy Wong, the only kid in their neighborhood with a mountain bike, sat next to Rosa. David Jaffe sat behind Sylvie. There was a new boy in their class, too. He had perfectly straight blond hair, wide blue eyes, and very white teeth. He looked like a kid in a toy commercial.

When Ms. McCracken finished the roll call, she sat down at her desk. It was very neat. "There are rules in this classroom," the teacher said. "If you follow them, we will get along nicely. If you don't, there *will* be consequences."

Sylvie's stomach started to hurt a *lot*. "I work all my students hard," Ms. McCracken went on. "I do not tolerate lateness, sloppiness, laziness, or disrespect. And I *never* tolerate misbehavior. Does everyone understand me?"

Ronnie Smith scowled down at her desk, but all the other kids in the class nodded. Sylvie wondered if she'd somehow wound up in prison instead of fifth grade. My parents *have* to get me transferred to Ms. Rivers's class, she thought. And maybe Carlos's parents will transfer him, too.

"This year, we're trying an experiment at Martin Luther King Elementary," Ms. McCracken said. "I will be teaching you social studies, math, science, health, and history. For ninety minutes every afternoon, the two fifth-grade classes will switch rooms. You'll go to Ms. Rivers's classroom, where she will teach you reading and English."

Sylvie felt a glimmer of hope. At least she wouldn't have McCracken all day long!

"And Mr. LaSalle will come by once a week for your music class," the teacher went on.

"Yay!" said David Jaffe. Sylvie remembered that David wanted to be a drummer when he grew up.

Ms. McCracken glared at him. "Mr. Jaffe, when you wish to speak in class, I expect you to raise your hand."

David's face turned bright red.

"I have one more announcement," Ms. McCracken said. "I would like to welcome a new student, Michael Leontes, to our school. Mr. Leontes's family just moved here from Los Angeles. Would you please stand up, Mr. Leontes?"

The blond-haired boy stood up, rolled his eyes, and sat down again. Carlos snickered, and Ms. McCracken raised one orange eyebrow at him.

Next the teacher went up to the chalkboard and wrote SOCIAL STUDIES in big letters.

"We will start social studies with class projects," she said. "You will each pick a partner. Then each team will build a model of a public space somewhere in this country. In three weeks, you will show the class your model and give an oral report on the place you chose."

Rosa Santiago put up her hand. "So we could build the Empire State Building?" she asked.

"Exactly," Ms. McCracken said, smiling. Sylvie could see it already—Rosa was going to get straight A's this year, too.

Kareem Jackson put up his hand next. Although his father had named him after a famous basketball player, Kareem was always the shortest boy in the class. "Could I open a window?" Kareem asked. "It's hot in here."

Ms. McCracken frowned. "*I* will open a window," she said. She raised the window and a cool autumn breeze blew into the room. Sylvie watched McCracken's teased orange hair. It didn't move a bit. She turned around and looked at Carlos, who grinned back at her. He'd been watching the teacher's weird hair, too.

"All right," Ms. McCracken said. "You may choose your partners and begin discussing a public space to work on."

Sylvie walked back to Carlos's desk. She saw Michael Leontes, the new kid, looking over at Carlos, too, but she got there first.

"Hey Sylvie, I've got the perfect thing for us to do," Carlos told her. "We can build Kennedy Airport."

Sylvie's mouth fell open. Kennedy Airport was one of the biggest airports in the country. There were miles of terminals and hangars and roads. "*All* of Kennedy Airport?" she asked.

Carlos thought for a second. "Maybe we'll just do one terminal near where my dad works." Carlos's father worked in air-traffic control. "We could use my model airplanes."

"Carlos, those planes are all from World War I," Sylvie reminded him.

"Oh, yeah," Carlos said. "Well, you can build the terminal and the runways. I'll make new airplanes. And we can get the information for the oral report from my dad. It'll be easy."

Ms. McCracken clapped her hands. "Quiet, please," she called. Then she started asking kids in the class what their partners' names were and what project they'd chosen.

When it was Sylvie's turn she said, "I'm working with Carlos Ortega. We're going to build a terminal at Kennedy Airport."

"With a runway and airplanes," Carlos added.

Ms. McCracken nodded and made a note on her clipboard. "Fine."

Sylvie looked at Carlos in shock. Fine?

"Told you it would be easy," Carlos mouthed.

"No talking, Mr. Ortega," Ms. McCracken said, without looking up. "Mr. Jackson, did you choose a partner?"

"I'm working with Sharon Fuller," Kareem answered. "We're doing the Grand Canyon."

"You can't build the Grand Canyon. It's not a building," Rosa Santiago protested.

"Ms. McCracken said it had to be a public space," Sharon said angrily from the back of the room.

Ms. McCracken frowned. "You are all talking out of turn," she said. "One more outburst and you will all have detentions." Then she turned to Kareem. "It might be easier to make a model of a building, Mr. Jackson, but the Grand Canyon certainly is a public space. You're welcome to try it."

Maybe this project wouldn't be so bad, Sylvie thought as the teacher went around the room. Ms. McCracken had approved almost all of the ideas.

A few minutes later, Ms. McCracken asked everyone to take out a pencil and notebook for math. Sylvie carefully took out her blue leather notebook.

"Nice notebook, Levine," Ronnie Smith whispered. Ronnie sat two seats away from Sylvie. "I'm going to get one just like it."

"You can't," Sylvie said. "It's really old. There isn't another one like it."

Ronnie smiled at her. "Then I guess I'll just have to take yours."

Sylvie didn't say anything back to Ronnie. But all during math and all through science she worried about what Ronnie had said. Sylvie had been planning to fill her new notebook with stories. Now Ronnie Smith would fill it with dumb Ronnie Smith things. Ronnie didn't even have good handwriting. She scribbled.

Finally, Sylvie couldn't stand it anymore. She tore off a small piece of notebook paper and wrote:

> *Ronnie's bugging me again.*
> *Meet me at my locker when*
> *Helmet Hair lets us out.*
> *　　　　—Sylvie*

Carefully, Sylvie folded the note and wrote Carlos's name on it. Then, making sure she kept her eyes on the front of the room, she passed the note to David Jaffe. She knew

David would pass it to Sharon, and Sharon would pass it to Carlos.

Sylvie was sharpening her pencil when she heard Ms. McCracken say, "Mr. Ortega, bring that piece of paper up to my desk. *Now.*"

Sylvie began to shake as Carlos took the note to the front of the room.

Looking a little pale, Carlos handed the note to their teacher. Ms. McCracken read it silently and frowned at Sylvie. She wished she'd never come to school that morning. She wished she'd never been born.

Finally McCracken said, "Mr. Ortega and Ms. Levine, I'll see you both after school today—in detention."

It was three thirty-five and Sylvie and Carlos were still sitting in Ms. McCracken's classroom. They were each writing "I will not pass notes in class" one hundred times. *Neatly.* Sylvie thought her hand was going to fall off.

She looked down at her paper. She was up to number eighty-three. Only seventeen more to go. Sylvie wanted to look at Carlos to see how he was doing, but she didn't dare. Finally, Sylvie finished her last sentence. She took the paper up to Ms. McCracken's desk. Carlos followed her a moment later. The teacher looked carefully at Sylvie's paper, then at Carlos's. She was counting the lines, Sylvie realized.

"I trust this will be the last time you two pass notes in my class?" the teacher asked sternly.

"Never again," Sylvie promised.

"No way!" Carlos agreed.

"Then you may collect your things and go," Ms. McCracken said.

Sylvie and Carlos wasted no time in getting their books and heading toward the door. Just as they reached the hallway, Ms. McCracken called after them, "Helmet Hair? Was that what you called me earlier?"

Sylvie couldn't be sure, but she thought she saw the teacher smile ever so slightly. "Uh..." she began. How was she ever going to explain this one?

"Go home, you two," Ms. McCracken said, her face stern again. "And I don't want to see either of you in detention tomorrow."

Sylvie and Carlos walked out of school fast. "I'm sorry I got you in trouble," Sylvie said.

"You ought to be," Carlos muttered, but Sylvie knew he wasn't angry. He put a hand on her shoulder. "It's no big deal. Roberto says *everyone* gets a detention with McCrackpot. We just got ours over with early."

"I hope so," Sylvie replied. Then she looked at her watch. "Oh, no!" she moaned. "It's almost four o'clock. We've already missed most of the soccer game."

Carlos shrugged. "Then we'll go cheer for

Kareem's team. He's a great player."

"So is Annie Tuzmarti," Sylvie said.

"You cheer for Annie, and I'll cheer for Kareem," Carlos said. "They're probably on the same team anyway."

That was one of the things Sylvie liked about being friends with Carlos. He was always reasonable.

They started across the schoolyard toward Harry Park. Carlos turned to watch a group of girls beneath the basketball hoop. They were shouting and kicking at something on the ground. "What's going on over there?" he asked.

"That's Ronnie Smith and her gang," Sylvie said. "Just keep going."

Carlos's face was grim. "Looks like they're picking on someone besides you this time. Let's see what's going on." He started toward Ronnie and her friends.

Sylvie stood for a moment, trying to decide what to do. The loyal part of her knew she should follow Carlos. The scaredy-cat part of her just wanted to run.

The loyal part won. Sylvie trudged after Carlos, her heart racing. She and Carlos could never stand up to Ronnie's gang.

Carlos came to a sudden stop. Ronnie and her gang weren't picking on another kid.

They were kicking at something small, furry, and terrified.

"It's a kitten!" Sylvie said, shocked.

"Let it go!" Carlos called loudly.

Ronnie whirled around. "You gonna make me?"

"You need to prove how tough you are by beating on a kitten?" Carlos said. He jerked his head toward Jodi and Cheryl and Juanita. "And you even need help. Four girls against a cat! Real impressive. This'll be all over school tomorrow."

"You won't live that long," Ronnie said. She stepped toward Carlos, her fists raised.

This is it, Sylvie thought, drawing back. *They're going to kill us. I'm going to die on the first day of fifth grade.*

"Tell you what," Carlos offered. "Leave the cat alone, and I'll take on all of you."

Ronnie smiled an evil smile. "All of us at once?"

"All at once," Carlos said.

"That's crazy!" Sylvie hissed to Carlos. "It's four against one!"

Carlos ignored her. "Deal?" he asked.

Ronnie looked at her gang. "Deal," they agreed. The girls had forgotten all about the kitten, which was cowering on the ground, shivering.

Carlos handed Sylvie his history book. "Hold this for me."

"So you can get killed?" Sylvie said, crossing her arms.

"Aw, come on," Carlos said.

Sylvie took the book. She wanted to close her eyes, but she didn't dare. This might be the last time she saw Carlos.

"Okay," Carlos said, turning to the four girls. "I'll fight you all. But first you have to catch me!"

In two seconds Carlos was racing across the schoolyard. And almost as fast, Ronnie and her gang were after him.

"We're going to destroy you, Ortega!" Ronnie screamed.

"Sylvie, the cat!" Carlos shouted.

Sylvie looked down. Huddled against the school's brick wall was the kitten. Its fur was muddy, but Sylvie could tell that it was mostly gray with a white chest, white paws, and a little white streak up the middle of its nose.

"Hey, kitten," Sylvie said, walking toward it.

The kitten's green eyes watched her. But as Sylvie moved closer, the little cat backed into a corner.

Sylvie stood perfectly still. "You're scared

of me," she said softly. "I don't blame you, after Ronnie was so mean. But I won't hurt you. I promise."

The kitten just looked at her and trembled.

"Nice kitty," Sylvie said, stepping toward the little animal again. "I'm just going to—" She stopped. What *was* she going to do? She couldn't take the kitten home with her. Her mother was allergic to cats.

Sylvie knelt down and held out her hand to the kitten. The kitten sniffed at her hand with its tiny pink nose. Sylvie smiled. It felt cold and wet.

"You're pretty scrawny," she said to the little cat. "I bet you're hungry."

The kitten rubbed its head along her hand.

"You want to be friends?" Sylvie asked.

The kitten rubbed her hand again.

Sylvie sat back on her heels and sighed. "I guess one friend has to make sure another friend doesn't starve," she said. She reached out and picked up the kitten. "Come on," she said. "Let's find you some dinner."

The little cat purred as Sylvie started home. What had happened to Carlos? Sylvie wondered. Had he escaped Ronnie and her gang? Carlos was one of the fastest runners in the school. Sylvie thought he had a pretty good chance. Now all she had to do was get home safely before Ronnie and her gang came back for her!

Sylvie walked along Grant Avenue, keeping her eyes open for Ronnie Smith. She had to walk very slowly so she wouldn't startle the kitten. Besides, she was having trouble balancing all those books and the kitten in her arms.

Sylvie had never walked so slowly in her life. It seemed as though it took forever to walk down Grant Avenue. But just as she reached Luigi's Pizza Parlor, Carlos stepped out onto the sidewalk. He was holding a paper plate with a slice of greasy-looking pizza on it.

"I've been waiting for you," he said, grinning. "What took you so long?" He reached up to scratch the kitten behind the ear. "Pretty cute cat. Is it a boy or a girl?"

"A boy, I think," Sylvie said. She handed Carlos back his history book. "How'd you get away from Ronnie?"

"Oh, I ran into the library. I knew those girls would *never* follow me there."

The kitten mewed in Sylvie's ear. She could feel its bony rib cage beneath her hand.

"This little guy needs food," she said. "What do kittens eat?"

Carlos shrugged and held out the paper plate to the kitten. "Pizza?"

The kitten sniffed at the pizza and licked it hungrily.

"Carlos," Sylvie said, "I don't think cats are supposed to have pizza."

"This one likes it," Carlos said. "I guess I'm not going to get any."

Now the kitten was tugging at the end of the slice, hard.

"We need some real cat food," Sylvie said.

"Let's go see Newton," Carlos suggested. "He sells everything."

A few minutes later, Carlos and Sylvie walked into Newton's narrow store. Newton was sitting behind the counter, listening to a small black radio.

"Do you sell cat food?" Sylvie asked. Even though Newton's store was mostly stocked with newspapers and magazines, there were lots of other things, too. Milk, soda, cookies, key chains, flashlights, aspirin, sewing kits— you never knew what you'd find at Newton's.

Newton nodded toward the back of the store. "Bottom shelf."

Sylvie and Carlos brought the food, a bag

of litter, and a blue litter pan to the counter. Sylvie wondered how much it was all going to cost. She had exactly two dollars in her pack. The supplies would probably cost a lot more.

"So," Newton said. "You're going to adopt this little cat? Which one of you is going to keep him?"

"Well, I can't," Sylvie said. "My mom's allergic."

"I can't, either," Carlos said. "Our landlord doesn't allow pets. We'll probably have to take him to the animal shelter, I guess."

"Carlos!" Sylvie said, shocked. "The shelter has to kill the animals it can't find homes for. What if no one adopts him?"

Carlos looked up at Newton. "Do *you* want him?"

Newton chuckled. "I've got three big, bad dogs at home. They'd eat this fellow for a snack." He leaned across the counter. "I'll tell you what," he said. "That starter kit there— the food and litter and pan—that's my gift to your kitten. Take a pet dish, too."

"Thanks a lot, Newton," Sylvie said.

Carlos and Newton slapped hands. "Thanks," Carlos said.

"We'll let you know when we find him a home."

"You do that," Newton said. "But find him

a name first. A fine little animal like that needs a name."

Sylvie and Carlos left the store. Sylvie carried the cat on her shoulder. Carlos carried the litter box, food, dish, and litter. "Now what do we do?" he asked as they set off toward Elm Street.

"We'll have to put up signs, I guess. But where can he stay until we find someone to adopt him?"

"There's only one thing to do," Carlos said. "We'll sneak him into my room. Maybe we can hide him there for a while."

Sylvie rolled her eyes. "Carlos, that's a terrible plan. Your parents aren't dumb. Of course they'll find out."

"Yeah, but maybe we'll find him a home first."

"Maybe," Sylvie agreed. "We've still got one more problem—what to name him."

Carlos smiled. "That's easy." He patted the little gray-and-white cat on the head. "What do you think of the name Newton?"

Sylvie and Carlos quickly put their plan into action. First Carlos called his house. Roberto answered the phone and told Carlos that neither of their parents was home. "Perfect!" Carlos said.

Then Sylvie called her mother from a pay phone to ask if she could stop at Carlos's for a little while before coming home. After she explained about Newton, Mrs. Levine said yes. Sylvie didn't mention that they were hiding the kitten from Carlos's parents.

Carlos's sister, Christina, opened the door. Christina had wavy black hair that fell to her waist. She went to high school and taught samba at Mrs. Ortega's dance studio.

"Where'd you get the kitten?" Christina asked, raising her eyebrows.

"His name is Newton," Sylvie said. "We found him in the schoolyard."

Roberto, Carlos's older brother, came up behind Christina. He took one look at Newton and another at Carlos. "Don't tell me you're going to try to keep that cat here," he said.

"Just until we find a home for him," Carlos answered.

"Carlos," Christina said gently, "cats make noise. Don't you think Mama's going to hear him?"

"It's just for a little while," Sylvie said quickly.

Roberto shook his head. Then he reached out and took Newton from Sylvie. "Come here, *gato,*" he said. "Let me show you your new home."

Christina went into the kitchen, but Sylvie followed the boys down the hall. The room that Carlos and Roberto shared was always a mess, but it was filled with great stuff. There were shelves of books and games. Model airplanes hung from the ceiling. A computer sat on Roberto's desk. Sometimes he let Sylvie and Carlos use it for computer games. Best of all, the ceiling was covered with a glow-in-the-dark map of the stars.

Roberto set Newton down on the floor, and Carlos poured some cat food into the new dish. The kitten wolfed it down, then watched curiously as Carlos set up the litter box.

"Don't put it under my desk!" Roberto warned.

"It's the only empty space on the floor," Carlos pointed out.

Sylvie looked around. There were clothes and sneakers and towels all over the place. Not really a place for a kitten, she thought. But it was definitely better than nothing.

The next morning Sylvie got up even earlier than she had the day before. Her mom and Willa were still asleep when she dressed, made her breakfast, and packed her lunch.

"Mom," she called out. "I'm going to school!"

Mrs. Levine came out of her bedroom, wearing her bathrobe. She looked very sleepy. "Why so early?" she asked.

"I'm stopping by Carlos's apartment this morning," Sylvie explained. "So I can visit Newton."

Mrs. Levine ruffled Sylvie's hair. "You never told me how your first day of school went. All you talked about last night was that kitten."

"School was terrible," Sylvie said.

"Terrible?" her mother echoed.

"Carlos and I got detention, so we missed

the soccer game. I already have tons of home-work from McCracken, and Ronnie Smith is going to beat me up," Sylvie reported. She quickly headed toward the door.

"Wait just a moment, young lady," Mrs. Levine called after her. "Why did you get a detention?"

"For passing a note," Sylvie said.

Mrs. Levine frowned. "We'll talk about this tonight," she said. "I certainly don't want you getting off on the wrong foot with Ms. McCracken."

"Okay," Sylvie said. If she was lucky, her mom would forget all about the detention.

She ran all the way from her building to the Ortegas' house.

Roberto answered the door this time. "*Qué pasa,* Sylvie?" he said. Roberto always liked to ask her "What's happening?" in Spanish.

" 'Morning, Roberto," Sylvie said. She low-ered her voice to a whisper. "How's Newton?"

Roberto grinned. "You don't have to whis-per," he said. "Newton introduced himself to my parents last night. Come on in."

Roberto led the way into the kitchen. Mrs. Ortega and Carlos were sitting at the table. Mr. Ortega had already left for work. Christina was probably in the bathroom, putting on makeup. She always looked great.

"Hello, everybody," Sylvie said. "Where's Newton?"

Mrs. Ortega nodded toward Carlos. He had the kitten on his lap.

"We're glad to see you, Sylvie," Mrs. Ortega said. "But please sit down. We need to talk about Newton."

Sylvie sat down at the kitchen table. She had a feeling that Carlos's mother was going to say that Newton had to leave.

"Sylvie," Mrs. Ortega began, "you know that we can't keep Newton in this building. If our landlord found out we had a cat here, he could ask us to move. No pets means no pets."

Sylvie looked down at the floor.

"You and Carlos are going to have to find Newton a home *quickly*."

"We know," Sylvie said in a small voice.

"And," Mrs. Ortega went on, "you have to understand that pets cost money. I'll take him to the vet and see that he gets a checkup and his shots. But I think you ought to help pay for his food."

Sylvie dug into her backpack. "I have two dollars," she offered. "It's all that's left from last week's allowance."

"And I have a dollar in my room," Carlos added.

Mrs. Ortega smiled. "All right. We'll all do

what we can to help. Christina's in the living room making up some signs for you. Why don't you go and see?"

Sylvie walked down the hall. Christina was sitting on the couch. The coffee table in front of her was covered with colorful flyers.

Sylvie picked up one of them. It said:

GREAT LITTLE CAT FOR ADOPTION
CALL CARLOS: 555-2941

"So what do you think, Sylvie?" Christina asked.

"They're—uh, excellent," Sylvie said. The flyers really did look good. There was even a little drawing of Newton in the corner of each one. And she didn't want to hurt Christina's feelings. But she didn't want to give up her cat, either.

"You and Carlos will get lots of calls," Christina said, sounding pleased.

Sylvie didn't know what to say, so she just thanked Christina and took some of the flyers. It wouldn't help things to be late for school. Ms. McCracken was waiting, like a black widow spider.

5

Sylvie stood in the schoolyard, holding a roll of tape. Beside her, Carlos was taping one of Christina's flyers to the side of the school building. "We'll put up a few here," he said. "This afternoon we can put some in Harry Park and a bunch on Grant Avenue."

Sylvie nodded. She was just about to hand Carlos more tape when she suddenly got a funny feeling. Someone was watching them. *Ronnie!* Sylvie thought.

She quickly turned around, but it wasn't Ronnie Smith behind her.

"Is anyone else out here covering school property with flyers?" Ms. McCracken demanded. In the sunlight, her hair looked even more orange.

"Uh—no," Sylvie answered. "Just us."

"Well, you can take them right down," Ms. McCracken said. "We do *not* deface school property at Martin Luther King, Jr., Elementary."

"There's already graffiti all over the wall," Carlos pointed out. "And these flyers are really important."

"What is important is that you do as I tell you," Ms. McCracken said. "*Now*. And I strongly suggest that you both behave yourselves in class today."

With that, the teacher walked briskly away. Sylvie saw that she was heading toward a sixth-grade girl who had thrown away her gum and missed the trash basket.

Carlos ripped the flyers off the wall. "This is not a great way to start the day," he said.

"And it can only get worse," Sylvie said, looking back over her shoulder at Ms. McCracken.

All through that morning, Sylvie worried. She worried about finding Newton a home. She worried about Ronnie Smith beating her up. She worried about McCracken thinking she was a troublemaker.

And then Sylvie got something new to worry about. She was working on a math problem when she heard Ms. McCracken say sharply, "Ms. Smith and Ms. Stein, we do *not* copy each other's papers in this classroom. I'll see you both in detention today. And Ms.

Smith, you may change seats with Mr. Jaffe. Permanently."

Sylvie's head shot up. David Jaffe sat behind *her!*

Ronnie scowled as she got her books together and changed places with David. Sylvie's heart began to pound, but Ronnie didn't say anything to her. She just opened her math workbook and began to draw a skull and crossbones on the inside cover.

Sylvie knew it was only a matter of time before Ronnie began to bug her. And it was all McCracken's fault!

Ronnie didn't wait very long. In science, Ms. McCracken was explaining how spiders spun their webs. *She probably knows all about that,* Sylvie thought. Suddenly, she felt something poke her in the back. She leaned forward in her seat. Then she felt another, harder poke. Sylvie turned around.

Ronnie Smith twirled her super-sharp pencil and smiled at Sylvie.

"Ms. Levine, may I please have your attention?" Ms. McCracken asked, frowning.

Two minutes later, Sylvie felt another poke, and then another. "Stop it!" Sylvie hissed.

"Ms. Levine." The teacher didn't even turn from the chalkboard. "You may join Ms. Stein and Ms. Smith in detention today."

Sylvie couldn't believe it. It was only the second day of school, and she'd already gotten two detentions! Behind her she heard Ronnie Smith chuckle. Why didn't McCracken hear *her?* Sylvie wondered. "Get used to it, Levine," Ronnie whispered. "And it's going to get worse."

At noon, Sylvie went to her locker to get her lunch, and looked around for Carlos. They always ate lunch together. But Carlos wasn't at his locker. She didn't see him anywhere in the hall, either.

She went downstairs to the cafeteria. Carlos was already there. He was sitting at a table with the new kid—Sylvie remembered that his name was Michael Leontes—and another guy in their class, Eric Holland.

Sylvie sat down with them. "How come you didn't wait for me?" she asked Carlos.

Michael Leontes gave her a strange look, but Carlos just shrugged. "Sorry, Sylvie."

"So what were you guys talking about before I came?" Sylvie asked, opening up her brown paper bag.

"Do you know anything about football?" Michael asked.

"Not a lot," Sylvie admitted. "My dad watches it on Monday nights."

Michael snorted and turned to Carlos. "Eric and I are going to scrimmage in the park this afternoon. Want to come?"

"I can't," Carlos said. "Sylvie and I have to do something."

Sylvie knew Carlos hated to play football. Roberto always gave him a hard time about it. Carlos said Roberto just wanted a chance to cream him. So Sylvie couldn't believe it when Carlos said, "Maybe tomorrow?"

"Cool," said Michael. "But you should stop by the park today anyway."

"Okay," Carlos said.

"What about putting up the flyers for Newton?" Sylvie asked him.

"You got a detention, remember?" Michael said. He pointed a straw right in Sylvie's face.

"I can put up my half of the flyers on my way to the park," Carlos said.

For the rest of lunch period the boys talked about football. Carlos acted like he was really interested. Sylvie couldn't understand why. Michael Leontes was a jerk.

When the bell rang, Sylvie was the first one up from the table. For once she didn't even wait for Carlos. She walked straight out of the cafeteria and headed back to McCracken's room.

She had just reached the stairway when she felt a hand close on her arm.

"Bet you're glad I'm sitting behind you now," Ronnie sneered.

"Let go of me," Sylvie said, trying to pull her arm away.

But Ronnie didn't let go. She smiled her nasty smile. "You and Carlos got off easy yesterday," she said. "One day soon it's going to be just you and me. And then I'm going to get you!"

That afternoon Sylvie had her second detention with McCracken. Ronnie and Jodi were there, too. They were supposed to write "I will not copy anyone else's paper" one hundred times, but Ronnie just stared out the window. Sylvie wrote "I will pay attention in class."

Luckily, Sylvie got out of the room first. She wondered whether McCracken would ever get Ronnie to write her sentences. Hopefully, Ronnie Smith would spend every single day after school in detention.

Sylvie started down Grant Avenue, looking for Carlos, but all she saw were a few of their flyers, posted on telephone poles and phone booths. There were enough of them up for now, she decided, so she went straight home.

Sylvie let herself into a very quiet apartment. No one was home. There were two notes on the refrigerator. One was from Joyce, Willa's baby-sitter. It said she and Willa were in the park. The other note was from Sylvie's mom. It said she had to work late at the store.

Sylvie sighed and wandered into the living room. She felt very lonely all of a sudden. Maybe she'd watch some TV.

She turned on the lamp in the living room. There was a big empty space on the rug where the big red velvet couch used to be. "Oh, Mom!" Sylvie said aloud with a groan. "Did you have to sell the *couch?*"

Sylvie sat on the rug and flipped on the TV. But there wasn't anything good on, and she began to feel restless.

Sylvie went into the kitchen and made herself a tuna-fish sandwich. Then she went outside to eat it on the front steps of her building. At least she could watch the people passing by on Elm Street.

Sylvie watched for Carlos as she ate her sandwich. She looked for Joyce and Willa, but she didn't see them, either. Everyone but her seemed to be in Harry Park. Sylvie thought of going to find Carlos, but she decided against it. Michael Leontes would be there, and she didn't want him to think she had no other friends. But it was true, Sylvie realized suddenly. Without Carlos, she was all by herself.

That night after dinner Sylvie read aloud to her mother and Willa. Then they all played a game of Monopoly. Willa kept running off with all the hotels, but that was okay with Sylvie. Their apartment seemed warm and cozy again.

But later, as Sylvie lay in bed, the lonely feeling she'd had after school came back to her. She wasn't used to feeling this way—all empty and hollow inside. She thought about Carlos suddenly wanting to play football with Michael Leontes. She thought about Newton spending the day alone in the Ortegas' apartment. *Tomorrow will be better,* Sylvie told herself as she drifted off to sleep. And, if she was really lucky, she wouldn't have any nightmares about Ms. McCracken and Ronnie Smith.

After school the next day, Sylvie and Carlos started to work on their project for Ms. McCracken. To Sylvie's relief, Carlos had told Michael he couldn't play football that afternoon, either.

Now Sylvie sat on the floor of Carlos's room, staring at a pamphlet about Kennedy Airport. It had a picture of the terminal she was supposed to build. The terminal had lots and lots of windows. "How do I make all these stupid windows?" she asked.

"Just cut them out, and use plastic wrap for the glass." Carlos began lining up the parts of a 747 jet.

Sylvie stared at the picture again. She had a feeling that her model was going to end up looking very different. She picked up a big piece of cardboard and began to draw windows with a felt-tip marker.

"Carlos," Sylvie said. "How come you're making all the planes, and I'm cutting out two hundred windows? You're getting to do all the fun stuff."

"Have you ever put together a model airplane?" Carlos asked.

"No," Sylvie admitted. "But I could learn."

"You sort of have to know how to do it," Carlos said. "My first models were terrible. You don't want to turn in something terrible to McCracken, do you?"

"No," Sylvie said. "I sure don't."

Suddenly a little gray-and-white paw darted out for the marker Sylvie was using.

"Hey!" Sylvie said. "Cut it out, Newton!" The kitten quickly retreated.

"I can't believe no one's called about him," Sylvie said. "Our flyers have been up for almost two whole days!"

Carlos looked up from his plane. "My mother says not that many people want to adopt cats."

"Well, I'm glad," Sylvie said. "I want Newton to stay."

Carlos didn't answer, but Sylvie knew that the cat couldn't stay at his house. Carlos began working on his airplane again. Newton batted around a tube of silver paint.

"We're almost out of cat food," Carlos said

finally. "This little guy eats a lot. And I already bought him more litter."

"I have five dollars saved in my bank," Sylvie said. "Maybe I can baby-sit for Willa."

Carlos took the tube of paint from Newton and squeezed some out on a piece of cardboard. Then he carefully began to paint the plane. "My dad said he might pay me to stop watching TV. I think he was kidding, though."

Sylvie heard the front buzzer ring. A few minutes later there was a knock on Carlos's door.

"Enter!" Carlos called.

Michael Leontes and Eric Holland came into the room. They were both wearing sweatpants. Eric had a football under his arm.

"Hey, Carlos," Michael said.

"Hi, Ortega," Eric said.

Neither of them looked at Sylvie.

Michael sat down on Carlos's bed and patted Newton on the head. "We're on our way to the park," he said. "You up for a game?"

"Sure," Carlos said eagerly. Then he looked over at Sylvie. "I mean, I guess I can't. Sylvie and I are working on our project."

"Do it later," Michael said. "It's going to

get dark soon. Now's the only time we can play."

The kitten crawled onto Michael's lap and began to purr. Sylvie didn't like that one bit. She didn't want Newton being nice to Michael Leontes. "Put him down, Michael!" she said.

Michael shrugged and set the cat down on the floor. "So Carlos, are you with us or not?"

Carlos looked down at his airplane. Then he looked at Sylvie.

"Carlos, we have to work on this project," Sylvie said.

Eric tossed the football up in the air. "It's not due for a long time."

Carlos nodded. "We can work on the model tomorrow," he told Sylvie.

"Carlos," Sylvie said, "you don't even *like* football!"

Carlos scowled at her. "I do so. You don't know what you're talking about." He got up and pulled on a sweatshirt.

"Wait a minute!" Sylvie said.

"What?" Carlos asked impatiently.

Sylvie needed a reason for Carlos to stay. "I—I never showed you what my father gave me." Quickly, she reached for her pack and pulled out the blue leather notebook.

"Big deal," Eric said.

"Yeah, borr-ring," Michael said.

Carlos looked at her like she'd lost her mind. "We've got to go now," he said.

Sylvie was too hurt to argue. All of a sudden, football was more important to Carlos than Newton or their project. Michael Leontes seemed to be more important than she was, too.

She watched the three boys troop out of the room. Carlos gave her a wave. "See you, Sylvie," he said.

"See you," she echoed.

Michael's voice carried down the hall. "So how come you hang out with a girl?"

"Sylvie's okay," Carlos said.

Okay? Sylvie fumed to herself. *Tell him I'm your best friend!*

Newton made a little *meep* sound and picked his way across the floor. He put a paw on Sylvie's knee.

Sylvie picked up the kitten and held him close. "Forget about Carlos," she told him. "You're my best friend now."

...Clarissa used her last wish. Poof! The magic ruby disappeared. But Clarissa had all the pets and friends she would ever want.

Curled up on her bed, Sylvie reread the story she'd written in her blue notebook. Then she wrote *The End* at the very bottom of the page.

She looked up as she heard a knock on her door. "Who is it?" she called.

"Guess!" a deep voice called back.

"Hi, Dad," Sylvie said.

Mr. Levine came into the room and gave her a kiss. Then he sat down on the chair at Sylvie's desk. "What's up, pumpkin?"

"I just finished a story for Ms. Rivers's class," Sylvie answered. "We had to write about someone who found a special wishing ruby."

Her dad smiled. "Well, that sounds pretty creative. But I wanted to ask you about something else. Your mom said that one of your classmates was going to beat you up."

"Ronnie Smith," Sylvie told him glumly.

"Again?" her father asked. "Didn't that boy threaten you in fourth grade?"

"Girl," Sylvie corrected. "She always threatens everyone."

Her father pushed his glasses up on his nose. "Well, does she actually *do* anything? Or does she just threaten?"

"She beat up Roger Pierson pretty bad last year," Sylvie said.

"I see," Mr. Levine said. "Maybe your mother and I should have a talk with Ronnie's parents."

"No!" Sylvie cried. "You can't do that! After Mrs. Pierson went to see Mrs. Smith, Ronnie beat Roger up again."

"All right," her father said. "Maybe it's your teacher I should speak to."

"That's an even worse idea!" Sylvie practically shouted. "Then Ronnie Smith will *kill* me. I'll be totally dead."

"Sylvie—"

"*Please*," Sylvie begged. "Just promise me you won't say anything to Ms. McCracken."

"I don't want you getting hurt," Mr. Levine

said firmly. "There has to be something we can do."

"I'll handle it, Dad. Trust me."

Mr. Levine leaned over and gave Sylvie a hug. "Maybe I'll talk to your mother about enrolling you in a self-defense class. 'Night, pumpkin."

" 'Night, Dad."

Sylvie didn't really believe she could handle Ronnie Smith—even with a self-defense class. But the last thing she needed was for her parents to talk to McCracken. Especially since she'd already gotten two detentions, and it was only September.

The next afternoon Sylvie read her story aloud in Ms. Rivers's class. Ms. Rivers was nothing like Ms. McCracken. Ms. Rivers was the nicest teacher Sylvie had ever had. She was young and wore her hair swept up in cornrow braids. And she wore perfume that smelled like springtime. Ms. Rivers wasn't strict like McCracken. In McCracken's class, everyone sat in perfectly straight rows. In Ms. Rivers's class, everyone sat in a circle.

"Thank you, Sylvie. That was wonderful," Ms. Rivers said when Sylvie finished reading her story.

Michael Leontes read his story next.

It was really short. His character wished for a surfboard, a race car, and a gazillion dollars.

"All right!" Eric said as Michael walked back to his desk. Carlos gave Michael a thumbs-up sign. No one had given Sylvie a thumbs-up sign.

Then Carlos read his story. His character used all three wishes for the same exact thing: He wished to be the best football player ever. Maybe all that banging around in the park had given Carlos brain damage, Sylvie decided.

"Annie, why don't you read next?" Ms. Rivers said.

Annie Tuzmarti made a face. She didn't like to be called on. Just then an office monitor entered the classroom. "Saved!" Annie said gleefully.

Behind the monitor was a pretty girl with coffee-colored skin and black hair that was pulled into a single thick braid. She wore a bright red dress. The monitor handed Ms. Rivers a file and left.

Ms. Rivers glanced at the file and smiled at the new girl. "Welcome," she said. "Everyone, this is Desdemona DuMonde. She just moved here from Manhattan and she'll be joining our class. Desdemona, would you like to tell everyone a little bit about yourself?"

"Sure," Desdemona said. She stood in front of the classroom with her chin pointed up. "The reason I'm starting school late is because my mother just finished doing a play in Connecticut. She's an actress."

Desdemona tossed her head so her braid swung around. "Everyone says I'm a born actress, too," she went on. "I was even named for a tragic heroine."

"A what?" Ronnie Smith said loudly.

"Desdemona is the name of a woman character in one of Shakespeare's plays," Ms. Rivers explained. "The play is called *Othello*."

"The bad thing is that Desdemona dies near the end of the play," Desdemona went on. "My mother played the role once in an all-black cast."

Ms. Rivers smiled. "I wish I'd seen that production."

"I know some of the lines," Desdemona said. "Do you want me to say them?"

"Please," the teacher said.

"This is from the scene where Desdemona is pleading for her life," Desdemona explained. "Then her husband, Othello, kills her."

Sylvie watched, fascinated, as Desdemona stretched out her arms and threw back her

51

head. For a moment she was silent. Then she spoke in a loud, clear voice. "'Alas, he is betrayed, and I undone!...Oh, banish me, my lord, but kill me not!...Kill me tomorrow; let me live tonight!'"

Everyone started clapping.

"Thank you, Desdemona," Ms. Rivers said. "Why don't you sit down next to Sylvie?"

Desdemona sat down, carefully arranging the pleats in her skirt. She smiled at Sylvie, and Sylvie smiled back.

Ms. Rivers asked some of the other kids to read their stories, but Sylvie wasn't really listening. She was thinking about what it would be like to have an actress for a mother. Sylvie tried to picture her own mom onstage. But all she could see was her mother standing in the kitchen in her red plaid bathrobe.

Sylvie came out of her daydream just as the bell rang. It was Friday afternoon and school was over. "Congratulations," Ms. Rivers said. "You've all survived your first week of fifth grade. School is closed on Monday and Tuesday for the Jewish holidays, so I'll see you again Wednesday afternoon."

Even though she figured it was a waste of time, Sylvie went to her locker and waited for Carlos. He'd probably go off with Michael and Eric today, too.

But Carlos showed up after all.

Sylvie gave him a big smile. "Ready?" she asked.

"I'm not going home," Carlos mumbled.

"What do you mean?"

"I've got to do something else."

Sylvie put her hands on her hips. "You said we could work on the project today."

"I know," Carlos said. "But now I can't. I've got to go to the dentist. How about tomorrow?"

"Okay," Sylvie said in a small voice. She watched Carlos walk off and join Michael Leontes down the hall. Was Carlos really going to the dentist? Sylvie didn't think so. But best friends didn't lie to each other, did they?

"Got you now, wimp!" whispered a voice behind Sylvie.

Sylvie spun around. Ronnie was always sneaking up on her.

"I'm gonna wipe the sidewalk with you, Levine," Ronnie crooned.

Sylvie shrank against the lockers.

"Me and my friends will be waiting for ya," Ronnie promised. She pounded a fist into her other hand. "The minute you step off the school grounds—*splat!*"

Sylvie watched Ronnie Smith lumber off toward the stairs.

She wished Carlos—or someone—was walking home with her. She wished she already knew self-defense. She wished she lived in another country.

I need a plan, Sylvie thought. *Fast.* Ronnie was waiting outside. There was only one thing to do, she decided finally. She'd just stay there until her parents sent the police looking for her.

Feeling better, Sylvie went back into Ms. Rivers's classroom. All the classrooms on the second floor were empty now. It was a little creepy being alone in the empty school, but Ms. Rivers's room felt friendly.

Sylvie sat down at her desk and waited. The classroom was very quiet. She could hear the clock on the wall and voices on the street below. She could even hear her own breath.

For a while she watched a sparrow in the tree outside the window. Then she watched the clock on the wall. The clock read three twenty, then three thirty, then three forty.

At four o'clock Mr. Hawkins, the school janitor, looked into Ms. Rivers's room. "Sylvie Levine, what are you doing here?" he asked.

"Waiting," Sylvie told him.

"I can see that," he said. "What are you waiting *for?*"

Sylvie felt silly saying she was waiting for her parents to call the police. And she couldn't tell Mr. Hawkins about Ronnie Smith, because then Ronnie would kill her for sure. So she said, "I'm just waiting."

"Well, you're going to have to wait outside," Mr. Hawkins told her. "I've got to lock up the school."

"Can't I stay a little longer?" Sylvie asked.

"No," Mr. Hawkins said firmly. "You cannot. Now let's go."

Sylvie wondered if there was someplace in the school she could hide. A broom closet, maybe. But Mr. Hawkins didn't give her a chance to look around. He walked her straight down the stairs and out the door. "Crazy kids!" Sylvie heard him mutter as he locked the door.

Sylvie walked to the edge of the schoolyard. She looked up the street and down the street. There was no sign of Ronnie or her gang. Sylvie was sure Ronnie hadn't given up. Maybe they were hiding in Harry Park. Or lurking in wait for her on Grant Avenue.

Now Sylvie was really worried. *Maybe I should take a different way home*, she thought. She could go the long way. But that meant walking by Parkside Cemetery. Sylvie shivered. She didn't believe in ghosts, but the cemetery was kind of spooky.

She didn't have a choice. Sylvie quickly headed away from Grant Avenue.

There was a storm on the way, and it was almost dark. A heavy wind swept through the trees in the park. Sylvie pulled her denim jacket tighter around her.

Sylvie walked all the way down Harrison South. Then she turned onto Taft Avenue. The cemetery was on Taft.

She stopped for a second as she passed an alley on the side of a red-brick apartment building. Had she heard something in the alley? It was probably her imagination, she decided. Then she heard it again.

"Been waiting for you." Ronnie Smith stepped out of the alley and crossed her arms. "I knew you were too much of a chicken to go down Grant."

Sylvie looked past Ronnie. She didn't see the usual gang.

Ronnie laughed. "I don't need any help to beat *you* up," she said. "This is going to be easy."

Ronnie took a step toward Sylvie. Sylvie backed away.

"Give me that blue notebook of yours," Ronnie demanded.

Sylvie kept backing up. They were getting closer to the cemetery now.

"I don't have the notebook," Sylvie lied. "I left it in my locker in school."

"Oh, yeah?" Ronnie said. "Then give me your pack. We'll just make sure you're not lying."

"I can't," Sylvie said.

"Why not?"

"Because—because the pack really doesn't belong to me," Sylvie lied again. "It's my sister's. If I go home without it, she'll kill me." She hoped Ronnie didn't know Willa was three years old.

Ronnie snorted. "Don't you get it? *I'm* going to kill you."

Sylvie backed right up to Parkside Cemetery's big iron gate. She heard the gate creak and felt it swing open behind her.

"This is perfect," Ronnie went on. "I get to

kill you and leave you in a cemetery."

Sylvie blinked back tears, and edged farther into the graveyard. She'd never been in a real fight before.

I need another plan, Sylvie thought frantically. *Maybe I can trip her or pull her hair or step on her toes—*

Sylvie stumbled and gave a little gasp. She'd run into a headstone!

Ronnie smiled her evil smile. In the growing darkness, the scar on her mouth looked like a bright white line. Ronnie always told everyone she got that scar fighting a pit bull. Sylvie believed it. Ronnie looked like she could mash any pit bull.

There was a crash of thunder.

"Say good-bye, Levine." Ronnie raised her fist just as a long, ghostly wail filled the air.

9

The terrible sound echoed through the old cemetery. Sylvie stood perfectly still. Even Ronnie seemed frozen to the spot.

The wail sounded again, high-pitched and bloodcurdling. *Could there really be a ghost behind that gravestone?* Sylvie thought wildly.

Ronnie's face was even whiter than her scar. "That must be the person they buried yesterday," she whispered. "I saw the funeral on my way to school." She pointed to a mound of fresh dirt a few feet away. "See?"

The ghostly cry echoed a third time. Ronnie turned and ran.

Sylvie knew she should get out of there too. But that meant running back through the graves. There might be other ghosts in the cemetery waiting to get her.

Then Sylvie heard a definite rustling behind a headstone. Her mouth dropped open as Desdemona DuMonde stepped out.

"I thought that would scare that Ronnie Smith off," Desdemona said, brushing her hands together.

"You scared me, too," Sylvie said.

"Well, I hate bullies," Desdemona said. "Besides, it was practice."

"For what?" Sylvie asked.

Desdemona grinned. "Oh, I don't know. The lead in a horror movie, maybe." She looked up at the sky. "We'd better go. It's going to rain soon. And my mother will throw a fit if I'm not there when she gets home."

"Mine, too," Sylvie said.

Together, they walked out of the cemetery. Desdemona stopped to shut the big iron gate.

"What were you doing in the cemetery, anyway?" Sylvie asked.

"Looking for graves of famous people," Desdemona answered. "Zoe Montgomery, the famous actress, is buried there."

"You're not afraid of being in there alone?"

Desdemona tossed her braid. "Nope. I'm scared of other things, though. Like dentists and robbers. Someone robbed our apartment when we lived in Manhattan."

"That's awful!" Sylvie said.

Desdemona shrugged. "Well, at least no one was hurt." She looked at Sylvie curiously. "So, where do you live?"

"On Elm Street, off Grant," Sylvie answered.

"I live on Oak," Desdemona told her. "Just two blocks away from you, I think."

As they walked Desdemona told Sylvie about the new play her mother was in. It was going to open at the Public Theater in downtown Manhattan. "And someday," Desdemona said, "I'm going to be an actress on Broadway."

"How do you know that?" Sylvie asked.

"I can feel it," Desdemona told her. "It's in my blood."

Sylvie looked at Desdemona with admiration. She had no idea what was in *her* blood besides oxygen and all the other things McCracken talked about in science class.

At the corner of Elm Street, Sylvie turned to say good-bye. "Thanks again for saving me," she said.

"Anytime," said Desdemona.

Sylvie headed home. She'd never met such a dramatic person before. She'd certainly never met anyone who visited cemeteries for fun. Desdemona DuMonde was okay. But she was definitely one of the strangest girls Sylvie had ever met.

On Monday morning, Sylvie and her family went to temple to celebrate Rosh Hashanah, the Jewish New Year. Sylvie was dressed in her best dress. It was navy blue with a wide plaid belt. Willa and their parents were dressed up too. On the High Holidays—Rosh Hashanah and Yom Kippur, the Day of Atonement—they always went to temple together.

Sylvie stirred restlessly in her seat. All around her, people were praying for a healthy new year. The rabbi who stood at the front of the room was praying in Hebrew, so Sylvie couldn't understand the words.

She couldn't wait till they blew the shofar. The shofar was a ram's horn, the same kind of horn that the ancient Hebrews had used. It didn't sound like the brass horns musicians played in bands. To Sylvie it sounded very old—like something calling from the past.

Sylvie looked down at her prayer book. It was early afternoon, and she felt as if the New Year's service had been going on all day.

Soon her mind began to drift. She thought about McCracken and Newton. And she thought about Carlos.

She still couldn't believe Carlos had dumped her to play football with dumb old Michael Leontes. She hadn't seen or heard from Carlos since. Nothing seemed to make sense. She *knew* Carlos didn't like football. And how could *anyone* like Michael? Carlos had never hurt her feelings before. What if Carlos was changing? What if he wasn't going to be her best friend anymore?

Tik-eeee—aaaah. Sylvie sat up as the first blast of the shofar filled the room.

The man standing in front of the ark blew two more times on the ram's horn, and the service continued. The rabbi made a speech about the New Year. Then different people got up to read from the scrolls of the Torah. Sylvie felt proud when each of her parents read. Once again, she didn't understand the Hebrew words, but she knew they were reading parts of the Bible.

Dusk was falling when services ended and the Levines started home for dinner. All over the neighborhood Sylvie saw other kids playing. Sylvie figured she ought to get two more days off from school for a real holiday.

Sylvie's father stopped as they passed the edge of Harry Park. "Isn't that Carlos?" he asked.

Sylvie looked. It was Carlos, all right. He was playing football with Michael Leontes.

Mr. Levine waved at Carlos. Carlos waved back. Then he ran over to see them.

"Hey, Sylvie," Carlos said. "Happy Jewish New Year."

Sylvie wasn't sure she wanted to talk to Carlos. She looked at him carefully. "What happened to your glasses?" she asked. "They're crooked."

Carlos reached up and touched the metal frames. "They got broken," he said. "Playing football."

"Your mom will kill you," Sylvie said.

Carlos shrugged. "It's a tough game. Listen, I've got good news. We found someone to adopt Newton."

"But weren't you going to keep him?" Mrs. Levine asked, looking puzzled. "I thought—"

"Who wants to adopt Newton?" Sylvie said quickly.

Carlos smiled broadly. "It's so cool. Michael Leontes."

Bright and early on Wednesday morning, Ms. McCracken took the roll. She seemed very pleased about something. Sylvie had already figured out that McCrackers looking pleased almost always meant trouble.

What's she going to have us do now? Sylvie wondered. *Build a model of the entire galaxy?*

"Class, I have an announcement," Ms. McCracken began. "Next Wednesday evening is a very special night. It's Parents' Night. All of your parents will have the chance to visit our school and meet the teachers."

Sylvie thought she was going to throw up. She could see it now. Her parents would walk into the classroom and McCracken would say, "Oh my, you're Sylvie Levine's parents. Ms. Levine is one of my worst students! I've already given her two detentions."

"We're going to decorate the classroom for your parents, of course," Ms. McCracken went on. "But first I want you to meet with your project partners. You are going to discuss two things: number one, what you have done so far on your project; number two, what you have left to do."

Sylvie and Carlos went to a corner of the classroom. Michael Leontes hadn't come to school today, Sylvie noticed suddenly. He hadn't taken Newton yet, either.

Carlos grinned at Sylvie. "This won't take long. What we've done is almost nothing.

What we still have to do is practically everything."

"Well, you know why," Sylvie said angrily. "Every time we're supposed to work on our project, you decide to go off with Michael Leontes."

"Aw, Sylvie, give me a break," Carlos said.

Sylvie crossed her arms over her chest.

Carlos sighed. "Okay, we'll work on the project today after school. Michael is out sick, anyway."

"I feel so lucky," Sylvie said.

"Sylvie!" Carlos said. "Cut it out!"

Sylvie felt herself getting madder and madder. "And there's one more thing," she said.

"What?"

"I don't want Michael adopting Newton."

"What's the matter with you?" Carlos asked, his voice growing louder. Sylvie saw Ms. McCracken heading toward them. "Newton needs a home, remember?" Carlos went on. "Michael is the only person who's offered to take him so far."

"Michael is a jerk," Sylvie hissed. The teacher was getting closer. "And I don't want my kitten growing up with a jerk!"

"*Your* kitten?" Carlos practically yelled.

Ms. McCracken was standing right over

them now. "Mr. Ortega and Ms. Levine, must I remind you that there is no shouting in this classroom?" she said.

Sylvie shut her eyes. She knew what was coming next.

"You may both see me after school today," the teacher told them. Then she walked away.

"Thanks a lot, Carlos!" Sylvie said, flouncing off toward her desk. She had just gotten her *third* detention, and Parents' Night was coming up fast.

That afternoon Carlos and Sylvie each wrote "I will not shout in class" two hundred times. When Ms. McCracken finally dismissed them, they went to their lockers without speaking.

"Well?" Carlos finally said.

Sylvie stared into her locker. "Well what?"

"Are we going to work on the project now or not?"

"Do you know what next Wednesday is?" Sylvie asked, putting her hands on her hips. "It's Parents' Night. Our parents are going to come to school to meet McCracken. And you know what she's going to say? 'Oh, you're Sylvie's parents. I've given Sylvie more detentions than anyone except Carlos.'"

Sylvie slammed her locker shut. "We're doomed."

"But Roberto's still got us beat," Carlos reminded her. "He had fourteen."

"Not by the second week of school!" Sylvie wailed. "If we keep going this way, we'll get two every week. That's more than thirty detentions by Christmas vacation!"

"Sylvie, chill out!" Carlos said, looking around.

"I hate McCracken," Sylvie said, slumping against the lockers. "And I hate fifth grade."

"Look," Carlos said, "I'm sorry about getting us in trouble. But it was your fault, too. Let's go to my house and work on the project. Okay?"

"No," Sylvie said. "You owe me an apology for more than arguing in class."

Carlos rolled his eyes. "I'm sorry if I hurt your feelings."

Sylvie was still a little mad at Carlos. He hadn't said he'd stop dumping her to hang out with the guys. But she wanted to be friends again. Besides, she had to see Newton before he went to live with that awful Michael Leontes. Then she'd never be able to visit him.

"Okay," she agreed finally. "Let's go build an airport."

Sylvie sat cross-legged on the floor of Carlos's room. She was dangling one of Roberto's sneaker laces in the air. Newton was trying to catch it.

Across the room Carlos held out a miniature 747. "Done!" he said proudly. "Our first plane. We just need three more."

Sylvie nodded toward the rectangular box in front of her. "I still have to paint the terminal and put in the windows. But at least I've got it put together."

The phone rang in another part of the apartment. A few minutes later Mrs. Ortega came into Carlos's room.

"Mrs. Leontes just called," she said. "She told me that she never gave Michael permission to adopt Newton. Michael's father hates cats."

Sylvie hugged the kitten to her. "So that means Michael can't adopt him?"

Mrs. Ortega nodded. "That's exactly what it means."

"Great!" Sylvie sang out.

"Sylvie," Mrs. Ortega said, "I know you don't want to give up Newton. But we can't keep him here."

"I know," Sylvie said with a sigh. "We'll find him another home."

"Well, please do it before he destroys my couch," Mrs. Ortega said. "He thinks it's a scratching post."

"The thing is," Sylvie said, "we have to find him a really good home. With people who will care about him as much as we do."

Mrs. Ortega bent down and picked up Newton, who was winding around her ankles. "I'm sure you'll do your best," she said. But Sylvie had a feeling Newton's days at Carlos's house were numbered.

The next day after school Carlos went off with Michael and Eric again. He didn't even tell Sylvie. She just saw the three boys heading for the park.

Desdemona DuMonde came up beside Sylvie. "Don't you and Carlos usually walk home together?"

"We used to," Sylvie said sadly.

"Want to walk home with me?" Desdemona asked.

"Okay," Sylvie said.

The girls started down Grant Avenue. For a while Desdemona was quiet. Then she said, "You and Carlos are pretty good friends, aren't you?"

"*Best* friends," Sylvie said. Then she added in a small voice, "Actually, I'm not sure about that anymore."

Desdemona nodded wisely. "Things change."

"But I don't want things to change," Sylvie said. "At least not with Carlos, anyway."

"Sometimes changes are good," Desdemona said. She grinned. "I mean, if things *didn't* change, we'd be stuck in McCracken's class forever. And you'd have detention for the rest of your life!"

"Very funny," Sylvie told her. "Wait until *you* have to stay after school with McCracken. I bet even Rosa Santiago will be in detention by the end of the year."

Desdemona stopped suddenly as they reached the stationery store.

"Let's go in here," she said. "I need to buy some colored paper for my project." Desdemona was making a model of the Delacorte Theater all by herself. The Delacorte was an

71

outdoor theater in Central Park where people watched free plays in the summer.

While Desdemona picked out the colored paper, Sylvie looked at notebooks. There weren't any as nice as her blue one.

Suddenly, she heard two familiar voices. Michael Leontes and Eric Holland were right down the aisle from her. Sylvie hoped they wouldn't see her. She knew Michael would say something mean.

Desdemona came up as Sylvie was sneaking away. "Shhh," Sylvie warned. She nodded toward the two boys.

Michael and Eric were looking at colored markers. Sylvie watched, amazed, as Michael grabbed a handful and stuffed them inside his jacket.

"Are you planning to pay for those?" Desdemona called.

Michael turned, his blue eyes angry.

"Maybe you ought to put them back," Desdemona said in a quieter voice. "Unless you want me to tell someone." She looked meaningfully toward the cash register.

"Mind your own business, DuMonde," Eric said.

"You're a worm," Desdemona replied, tossing her braid.

Michael put back the markers. "You better

not squeal," he said, trying to sound tough.

Desdemona brushed past him and Eric. "Come on, Sylvie," she said. "Let's *pay* for our things and get out of here."

Michael and Eric left the stationery store first. Sylvie waited while Desdemona bought her colored paper.

She didn't say very much as they walked home.

"What's the matter?" Desdemona asked after a while.

"I was thinking about Carlos," Sylvie said. "I wonder if he knows his new best friend is a thief."

On Tuesday morning Ms. McCracken made another announcement. "Your projects are due one week from Friday," she said. "So today each team will give us a progress report."

Sylvie's and Carlos's eyes met. Sylvie looked away. She and Carlos hadn't made much progress on their project at all.

"Who wants to go first?" Ms. McCracken asked.

Rosa Santiago waved her hand. *Of course,* Sylvie thought when the teacher nodded.

Rosa and her partner, John Jerome, walked to the front of the room. "John and I are doing the Washington, D.C., monuments," Rosa began. "Almost all of them."

John nodded. It was clear that Rosa was going to do all the talking. Knowing John, Rosa was probably doing all the work, too.

"We already built the Washington Monument and the Lincoln and Jefferson memorials," Rosa said. She reached into the pocket of her sweater. "I brought Polaroids."

Sylvie saw Carlos put his head down on his desk.

Rosa passed around her snapshots. They showed perfect-looking models of the monuments. The Lincoln Memorial had a tiny statue of Abraham Lincoln and even tinier visitors.

Sylvie groaned. Maybe Rosa had come from another planet. A planet full of perfect students just like her. The girl just couldn't be human.

"We're not done yet," Rosa went on. "We still have to build the Vietnam Wall."

Ms. McCracken handed the photographs back to Rosa. "Very nice," she said. "Keep up the good work."

Ms. McCracken called on Michael and Eric next. They talked about their model of Shea Stadium, where the New York Mets played. Michael seemed to like baseball even better than football.

Ms. McCracken didn't look quite as pleased with their report. But she didn't say anything bad about it.

Kareem and Sharon talked about their model of the Grand Canyon. Sylvie couldn't tell how much work they'd actually done. Kareem gave names for different layers of rock. Sharon just kept saying, "And it's really big!"

Annie Tuzmarti and Sasha Sommers were next. "Our model is of the south end of Harry Park," Sasha said in her soft voice. "We're building the bandstand and the duck pond. We still have to do the bicycle paths."

"And we're adding something else," Annie broke in. "It was in the park in 1925, but it isn't there now."

"How interesting," Ms. McCracken said. Then she looked straight at Carlos and Sylvie.

"Mr. Ortega and Ms. Levine," Ms. McCracken said. "How is Kennedy Airport coming along?"

"Great," Carlos said quickly. "Flights are arriving and departing all the time."

Ms. McCracken didn't think that was funny. "Why don't you two come up and tell us about it?" she said, frowning.

Sylvie got up from her desk and walked to the front of the room. Carlos was right behind her. Sylvie turned and looked at him helplessly.

Carlos started talking. "I made a model of a 747 jet," he said. "And Sylvie started the terminal."

"That's all you've done?" Ms. McCracken asked, raising her eyebrows.

"Sylvie's done a *lot* of work on the terminal," Carlos said.

"Ms. Levine, which is it?" the teacher asked. "Did you and Mr. Ortega just start your project? Or have you done a lot of work?"

Sylvie knew she couldn't lie to a teacher. Especially Ms. McCracken. "We just started," she said in a very small voice.

"I don't approve of procrastination," Ms. McCracken said, tapping her pencil on the desk. "That means putting things off till the last minute."

"We'll work on the model again today," Sylvie promised.

"I hope so," Ms. McCracken said. "And I'll be expecting some real work to be done!"

At noon, Carlos ate lunch with Michael and Eric again, so Sylvie sat with Desdemona. As soon as the girls were done eating, they went outside to the schoolyard.

They were just about to join a game of kickball when Carlos came over to Sylvie. Michael Leontes was with him. "Uh, Sylvie, we have to talk," Carlos said.

"What about?" Sylvie asked.

"You told McCracken we'd work on our project today. Well, I can't."

Michael put an arm around Carlos's shoulder. "Ortega and I have plans."

Sylvie wondered if Michael was planning to go to a store and steal something. But she couldn't say that. Not with Michael standing right there.

"Your plans are bad news," Desdemona told Michael.

"You'd better shut up," Michael told her, stepping forward.

"Listen, Sylvie," Carlos said, "we'll work on the model some other time, okay?"

"Carlos," Sylvie said, "tomorrow night is Parents' Night. Just what do you think McCracken is going to tell our parents?"

Michael yawned. "Who cares?"

Sylvie threw up her hands in exasperation. "If we don't do a good job on this project, we're really going to be in trouble."

"It's no big deal," Carlos said. "We've got

over a week. That's lots of time left."

Sylvie counted silently to ten and took a deep breath. "*When* will we work on it?" she asked.

Carlos shrugged. "I'll call you. Okay?"

"No, it is *not* okay!" Sylvie yelled. She didn't care if every kid in the schoolyard heard her.

Desdemona stepped in front of Sylvie. "I thought you were Sylvie's friend," she said to Carlos, putting her hands on her hips.

"Ortega doesn't hang with girls," Michael said.

"And *you* are the lowest life form on the planet!" Desdemona told him. "Lower than McCracken's gross bugs."

Sylvie tried again. "Carlos," she said.

Michael started to laugh. "She's so dense," he said to Carlos. "She just doesn't get it."

"Get what?" Sylvie demanded.

"Even a first-grader would get the message," Michael said. "Tell her, Ortega!"

Carlos looked at the ground. "Get lost, Sylvie. Just get lost!"

That night Sylvie went to bed right after dinner. She didn't want to talk to anyone. She still couldn't believe Carlos had been so mean to her! He wasn't her best friend anymore. He wasn't any kind of friend at all.

Sylvie huddled beneath the covers. It was only seven o'clock, and she wasn't sleepy. Normally she didn't go to bed until nine. But she needed some time alone to think.

She had a lot to worry about. Newton still needed a home. Tomorrow was Parents' Night. Carlos was best friends with a no-good thief. And now they'd never finish their project for McCracken. Because she was never going to speak to Carlos Ortega again!

"Sylvie!" her dad called. "Telephone for you."

"If it's Carlos, tell him I'm dead!" Sylvie called back.

Mr. Levine stuck his head in the doorway. "It's a Miss Desdemona DuMonde," he said. "Would you like me to tell *her* you're dead?"

"No," Sylvie said with a sigh. She got out of bed and answered the phone.

"Hi," Desdemona said. "Do you want to come over to my house tomorrow after school?"

"Um, sure," said Sylvie. "I guess I'm not going to be working on my model with Carlos."

"He's a jerk," Desdemona said.

"He's not a jerk," Sylvie said at once. For some reason, she couldn't let anyone else call Carlos names. "Let me ask my mom about tomorrow," she added, and ran down the hall. "Everything's cool," she told Desdemona a few moments later.

After Sylvie hung up the phone, she went straight back to her room. A few minutes later her mother knocked on her door and came in. "What's wrong, sweetie?" Mrs. Levine asked. "You're not sick. And this is too early for your bedtime."

"It's a long story," Sylvie said. "I don't really want to talk about it. Mom, you and Dad aren't going to Parents' Night tomorrow, are you?" Yesterday, Ms. McCracken had given them all a notice to bring home.

"Of course we are," her mother answered.

"But don't you have a lot of work at the store?" Sylvie asked hopefully.

"There's always a lot of work at the store," Mrs. Levine said. "But you know we'd never miss Parents' Night."

"It'd be okay if you missed it this year," Sylvie assured her. "It's no big deal. Really. I'd understand if you guys are too busy."

Mrs. Levine smiled. "That's very sweet of you. Now, why don't you want me to meet your teachers?"

"Oh, I do!" Sylvie lied.

Her mother sat down on the bed beside Sylvie and brushed a strand of Sylvie's hair back from her face. "Honey, are you in some kind of trouble?"

"No," Sylvie said in a small voice. She just couldn't tell her mom how terrible everything was.

"Why did you ask your dad to tell Carlos you were dead?"

"Because I'm never speaking to Carlos ever again."

"Well, what about Newton?" her mother asked. "How are you going to take care of him if you're not speaking to Carlos?"

Sylvie buried her face in the pillow. "I don't know," she mumbled.

"And what about all the things you and Carlos always do together?"

"They're over," Sylvie said. "Me and Carlos are history."

The next morning, Sylvie and her father had breakfast together. Willa and Mrs. Levine were still asleep.

Mr. Levine coughed a little as he finished a piece of toast. Quickly, he took a sip of coffee.

"Dad," Sylvie said, "you don't sound so good. Maybe you and Mom should stay home tonight."

"Sylvie, I'm fine," her father said.

"But Mr. Ortega isn't," Sylvie lied again. "He's got a really bad cold. If you and Mom go to Parents' Night, you might catch his germs and get *really* sick."

Sylvie's father frowned. "Luis Ortega is a very sensible man. I'm sure that if he's that sick, he'll stay home."

"He might not," Sylvie said.

"Sylvie, what's the matter?" her father asked.

Sylvie shrugged. "Nothing. It's just that you've already been to five Parents' Nights, if you count kindergarten. They must be getting kind of boring."

"Never," her father said. "I always find them very interesting. Besides, I'm curious to meet this McCracken woman. She sounds like a very dedicated teacher."

"Dad!" Sylvie moaned.

Mr. Levine folded his newspaper. "Don't worry, pumpkin. I'm sure your mother and I will have a very nice talk with Ms. McCracken."

All day long at school, Sylvie was a wreck. Every time she looked at Ms. McCracken, she thought about Parents' Night. And she had to see Carlos in class.

Sylvie tried to pretend her ex–best friend wasn't there. She didn't even look at him. Carlos didn't look at her either. And he certainly didn't talk to her. Michael and Eric ignored her, too.

After school, Sylvie went home with Desdemona. "Are your parents going to Parents' Night?" Sylvie asked as they started down Oak Street.

"My dad's not around," Desdemona said easily. "He and my mom split up when I was a baby. We're not that close."

"Oh," Sylvie said. "How about your mom?"

"She can't go," Desdemona answered. "She has a rehearsal in the city tonight."

"You are so lucky," Sylvie said.

Desdemona looked at her curiously. "Why? I always want her to go to things at school, and she hardly ever can."

"I bet you anything all the parents will think McCracken's great," Sylvie said, kicking at a bottle cap.

"My mom can always tell when someone's acting," Desdemona said. She started up the stairs of a blue three-story building and let them into the second-floor apartment.

Sylvie looked around. The DuMondes' apartment wasn't filled with old stuff like hers. Everything looked bright and new and sleek. Colorful posters for plays were framed on the wall. Big green plants filled the windows.

Sylvie followed Desdemona into the kitchen. Desdemona checked the clock. "My mother has a costume fitting this afternoon," she said. "She'll be home soon."

Desdemona walked over to the refrigerator and offered Sylvie a soda. "Want to dress up?" she asked.

"For what?" Sylvie asked, looking down at her jeans.

"Come on," Desdemona said. She led Sylvie to a small room off Mrs. DuMonde's bedroom. "This is the dressing room," she said proudly. She pointed to a table with a mirror over it. "Have a seat," she said. "We'll start with makeup."

"Your mother lets you use makeup?" Sylvie asked, amazed. Her mother said she'd have to be forty before she could use makeup.

"Only inside the apartment," Desdemona answered. She picked up some makeup brushes from the table and squinted at Sylvie. "Hold still," she said.

Desdemona dusted a thick white powder over Sylvie's face. Then she brushed blue eye shadow on Sylvie's eyelids. Next, she put glittering golden stars on her cheeks. Finally, Desdemona opened the dressing-room closet and took out a long, silky gold robe. "Put this on," she said.

"Won't your mother be mad?" Sylvie asked. "My mom hates it when I wear her clothes."

"This is just an old costume," Desdemona explained. "I'm always allowed to play with old costumes."

Sylvie slipped on the golden robe while Desdemona made up her own face. Then she put on a long blue dress with rhinestones. The two girls looked at each other in the mirror.

"We're fabulous," Desdemona said. "Let's dance."

"Dance?" Sylvie said blankly.

Desdemona ran into the living room and put a compact disk into the CD player. The sounds of an orchestra filled the living room. "Vivaldi wrote this music," Desdemona said. "He's very cool."

"Oh," Sylvie said.

Desdemona held her arms over her head, closed her eyes, and began to dance. She moved in exact time with the music. Sylvie kept her eyes open and tried to do the same thing.

"We're trees in a rainstorm," Desdemona cried. She bent to the side, swinging her arms. "Now we're stars whirling through the sky." She opened her eyes and spun across the rug.

Sylvie laughed and followed along. It was silly but fun. Together the girls were trees and stars and grass on the prairie. They were being the ocean during a storm when Mrs. DuMonde came home.

"My, my," said Desdemona's mother as she opened the door. "What have we here?"

"The ocean," Desdemona called.

Sylvie stopped dancing altogether. She'd never seen anyone as exotic-looking as Desdemona's mother. Mrs. DuMonde's eyes were made up with shiny silver paint. Her black hair was piled high on top of her head. She wore a long, swirling purple skirt over a black leotard.

She smiled at Sylvie. "Are you the ocean, too?"

Sylvie looked over at Desdemona. Her friend was still whirling about, rising and falling with the music. "I think I'm just a wave," Sylvie said. "Sort of a calm one."

Mrs. DuMonde held out her hand. "Well, I'm pleased to meet you. We could use a calm wave around here."

Desdemona stopped whirling. "Angie, this is Sylvie Levine. Sylvie, this is my mother, Angeline DuMonde."

"You can call me Angie, too," the actress said as Sylvie's mouth dropped open. "We're not formal around here. You must be the girl who's having boy trouble."

Sylvie felt herself turning red. "You told her about Carlos?" she asked Desdemona.

"Of course," Desdemona answered. "Angie and I talk about everything. You aren't mad, are you?"

"Don't feel bad, Sylvie," Mrs. DuMonde said. "Things like this happen all the time. People can be best friends one day, and the next day they've both changed. Sometimes it's for the best."

"*I* didn't change," Sylvie said. "Carlos did. And why should I have to change just because he did? It's not fair."

"No one ever said it was fair, honey. The truth is, there's not much you can do about it. If Carlos needs to go off with other friends, then you've just got to let him go."

"But he's wrecking things for her in class," Desdemona said. "Ms. McCracken will flunk both of them if they don't finish their project."

"I can't work with Carlos anymore," Sylvie said sadly.

Mrs. DuMonde spoke in her deep, rich voice. "Well, it sounds as though there's only one solution, Sylvie. You're going to have to finish the project on your own."

"I guess you're right," Sylvie said with a sigh. "But I still say it isn't fair."

The next morning Sylvie didn't get out of bed right away. Last night her mom and dad had met Ms. McCracken at Parents' Night. Which meant today they were going to be really mad at her.

She heard a knock on her door and then her mother's voice. "Sylvie, time to get up. You don't want to be late for school."

Yes, I do, Sylvie thought. *I'm never going to school again.* She wasn't sure whether her mom had sounded angry. Just in case, she was never going downstairs again, either.

Fifteen minutes later, Sylvie's mother came into her room. She looked mad, all right. "Sylvie, why aren't you up?"

"I'm sick," Sylvie mumbled.

Her mother crossed her arms. "Oh, really? What's the problem?"

"My stomach hurts. And my head."

Mrs. Levine went over and put her hand on Sylvie's forehead. "Nope. You don't have a fever. Does this by any chance have anything to do with Parents' Night?"

Sylvie gulped. "What did Ms. McCracken say about me?"

Mrs. Levine sighed. "She said you were a good student who could do better."

"That's all?" Sylvie asked, sitting up in bed.

"That's all," her mother answered. "Now get dressed and come to breakfast. You can start doing better by getting to school on time."

That afternoon Sylvie and Desdemona walked home from school together again. "So what did old Crack-the-Whip McCracken tell your parents last night?" Desdemona asked.

"Nothing too awful," Sylvie said. "The worst thing is they thought she was wonderful. My dad kept saying she was a good old-fashioned teacher. And my mother thought she was lovely."

"Lovely?"

Sylvie nodded. "Can you believe it? They think I'm lucky to have McCracken."

Desdemona shifted her book bag to her

other shoulder. "Parents are weird some-times."

"Tell me about it," Sylvie agreed.

They passed Roberto and a bunch of his friends, hanging out in front of the corner store. "*Qué pasa,* Sylvie?" Roberto called out.

"Hey, Roberto!" Sylvie called back, giving him a wave.

"Who's that?" Desdemona asked.

"Carlos's brother. He's pretty nice to me."

"So have you decided what to do about Carlos?" Desdemona asked.

"No," Sylvie replied. "But I am going to finish the project on my own, like your mom said. The problem is, I don't know how to build model airplanes. And even if I did, I don't have the parts. Everything is in Carlos's room."

"Then you have to get them," Desdemona told her. "If Carlos can make a model, then so can you."

"It looks pretty hard," Sylvie said.

"Just go and get all the stuff," Desdemona said. "Besides, Carlos won't care. He's not going to work on that project anyway."

After she and Desdemona said good-bye, Sylvie walked down Elm Street and stopped in front of the Ortegas' building. She was pretty sure Carlos wasn't home. He and

Michael had left school together.

Sylvie marched up the stairs and rang the Ortegas' bell. No one answered. She rang it a second time, then a third. After a few more tries she gave up. No one was home.

Sylvie sat down on the steps to wait. She didn't have anything else to do anyway. She watched Mr. Jeffers, who lived up the street, walk his dog. She watched her next-door neighbor, Mrs. Costa, come home from work. She watched a car circle the block, looking for a parking space.

"Hi, Sylvie." Christina was standing at the bottom of the stairs. "What are you doing here?"

"I need to get something from Carlos's room," Sylvie said. "And no one was home. I rang the bell five times."

"What do you need?" Christina asked.

Sylvie wondered how much she should tell Carlos's sister. What if Christina wouldn't let her take the models? But Christina guessed what Sylvie wanted.

"You need that terminal you're building?" she asked.

"And the airplanes."

Christina looked surprised. "Isn't Carlos making all the planes?"

"Carlos doesn't want to work with me anymore," Sylvie said. "He has a new best friend now. Michael Leontes."

"That kid with the blond hair?"

"That's him," Sylvie said. "Michael doesn't like me. And Carlos told me to get lost."

"I can't believe that," Christina said, frowning.

Sylvie blinked back tears. She knew she sounded like a baby. "Carlos spends all his time with Michael now. I haven't even seen Newton for days!"

Christina put a hand on Sylvie's arm. "Come on," she said gently. "I'll let you in."

Sylvie followed Christina up the stairs and into the apartment. Christina turned on the lights in the living room. Newton was sleeping on the couch. He opened his green eyes and blinked.

"Newton, I missed you!" Sylvie said. She ran over to the couch to give the kitten a hug. Newton purred when she picked him up. "Has anyone called about adopting him?" Sylvie asked.

"No one," Christina answered.

Sylvie cradled the cat in her arms. "I think he's getting bigger."

"He ought to be," Christina said. "He eats as much as Roberto." Then she frowned. "Sylvie, do you hear something?"

Sylvie listened. She *did* hear funny noises. "It sounds like it's coming from Carlos's room," she said.

Christina went down the hall to Carlos's room, motioning Sylvie to stay quiet. Sylvie followed her nervously. Had robbers broken into the Ortegas' house?

Soon Sylvie could hear high beeping noises, the kind a computer made. Then she heard voices, and someone laughing. Someone who sounded like Carlos.

Christina and Sylvie peered inside the bedroom. Carlos and Michael Leontes were sitting at Roberto's computer, playing a game. They were so caught up in the game, they didn't even notice Sylvie and Christina. "Why didn't you answer the doorbell?" Christina demanded. "Sylvie rang it five times."

Carlos looked up. "Sorry. We didn't hear it."

Christina glared at her brother. "Do you know why Sylvie is here?"

Carlos shrugged. "You want to play a computer game?" he asked Sylvie.

"No," Sylvie told him. "I'm taking our project. I'm going to finish it myself."

"You can't," Carlos said. "You don't know how."

"I'll figure it out," Sylvie snapped. She reached down and grabbed the model of the terminal building. Then she began grabbing airplane parts and tossing them inside it.

"Sylvie, cut it out," Carlos warned.

"What do you care?" Sylvie asked. "I hope McCracken gives you an F on this project. I hope you flunk the whole fifth grade!"

Michael gave Carlos a nudge. "Are you going to let her steal your stuff like this?"

Sylvie threw the finished model of the jet in the box. "Shut up, Michael. *You're* the one who steals!" She snatched up the tube of silver paint. "I just wish I could take Newton, too. Because I'm never going to speak to you again, Carlos Ortega!"

"You just lucked out," Michael told Carlos.

"Fine!" Sylvie took her box and stomped from the room. Christina ran after her, but Sylvie was out of the apartment before anyone could stop her.

Sylvie stared at the parts of the tiny passenger jet that were spread out on the living-room table. She was sure she could put together one itty-bitty jet. But she'd been working on it for over an hour.

Mr. Levine looked up from his newspaper.

He liked to read the sports pages at night. "How's it going, pumpkin?" he asked.

"Awful," Sylvie told him.

Her father came over to the table. "What seems to be the problem?"

"I think I'm missing some parts. See? I've got two wings and the body. But no engines and no landing gear."

"Hmmmm..." Mr. Levine said, stroking his chin.

"Dad, that's not helpful," Sylvie told him.

"Well, how about looking at the directions?" her father suggested.

Sylvie threw up her hands. "I left those at Carlos's, too. And I'm not going back to get them!" She tossed a piece of the plane across the table. "Airplane models are so dumb!"

"That may be," her father said. "But it won't help you finish your project."

"Maybe I'll just drop out of fifth grade," Sylvie said.

"Sylvie!" Mr. Levine warned.

"Oh, all right," Sylvie said with a sigh. Then the doorbell rang, and she looked up hopefully. "Did you send out for pizza?"

"No." Her father went over to answer the buzzer, and a few moments later he opened the door. Carlos was standing there, shifting from one foot to the other.

"Hi, Mr. Levine. Is Sylvie around?" he asked.

Mr. Levine stepped away as Sylvie came to the door. "I'm not talking to you," she said, folding her arms.

"Sylvie, I'm sorry," Carlos said. "I still want to be friends."

"You told me to get lost in front of the entire school!"

"It wasn't the entire school," Carlos said, rolling his eyes. "But I didn't mean it."

"Are you still friends with Michael?" Sylvie asked.

"What's that got to do with anything?" Carlos demanded. "Look, I'll take care of Leontes. I won't let him be mean to you again. And I won't be, either. Honest."

Sylvie shook her head. "If you hang out with that creep, then you can't hang out with me."

"That's crazy," Carlos said. "You can't go telling people who to be friends with. Besides, we have to finish our model."

So that was it. Carlos was just worried about McCracken's project. "Go work with Michael!" Sylvie snapped. Then she slammed the door in Carlos's face, good and hard.

13

"Use this," Willa said, handing Sylvie a piece of plastic wrap for a window. It was Saturday morning, and Sylvie was trying to finish the model for McCracken's class.

"Later," Sylvie said, handing the plastic back to Willa. "Just hold that for a minute."

"No," Willa said. "Use it now."

The doorbell buzzed, and Sylvie jumped up to answer it. "Who's there?" she called into the intercom.

"Roberto."

Sylvie buzzed him up. When she opened the door, Roberto stood smiling at her. He was holding a paper bag in one hand. "*Qué pasa,* Sylvie?"

Sylvie nodded toward the living-room table. "Guess."

"It's not going so well, huh?"

Sylvie shook her head. "I haven't even

gotten one stupid plane together!"

"I thought maybe I could help," Roberto said. "I've got the rest of the parts and the instructions."

"That would be great," Sylvie said.

Roberto sat down at the living-room table. Sylvie watched as he showed her how to put a model together. It didn't seem so hard, really.

"Sylvie, listen," Roberto said finally, putting down the plane. "I know Carlos hasn't been acting very cool lately."

"He's been a jerk!" Sylvie said.

"Yeah," Roberto agreed. "But hey, that doesn't mean he's stopped being your friend. It's just sometimes a guy needs to hang out with other guys, you know?"

"You're the one who's always telling him he's not tough enough," Sylvie pointed out.

"Yeah, well, maybe I should lighten up a little," Roberto said. "But what I'm trying to tell you is that just because Carlos acts like a turkey, doesn't mean he doesn't like you anymore."

"His big buddy Michael doesn't like me," Sylvie said.

"Hey, I don't like that guy much either," Roberto told her. "He looks like trouble to me. But you really ought to give Carlos another chance. He's okay most of the time. Besides, you two have to do something about that cat. Our landlord saw him when he came by yesterday to collect the rent."

"What happened?" Sylvie asked quickly.

"He gave the cat one week."

Sylvie gulped. Only seven more days! If nobody offered to adopt Newton, it was the animal shelter for sure.

Roberto stood up. "I've got to be going. But give Carlos a call, okay?"

"Thanks, Roberto," Sylvie said.

"Any time," Carlos's brother replied. He reached over and tweaked Willa's nose. "See you, *chiquita*."

"*Adiós*," Willa said.

Roberto laughed. "*Adiós*," he replied.

That afternoon Sylvie met Desdemona at Chang's Chinese Restaurant. Outside, rain streaked the window and made the street look shiny, but inside the restaurant was warm and cheerful.

A waiter came over to their table. They each ordered an egg roll and a cup of wonton soup. Eating at Chang's had been Desdemona's idea. She ordered takeout from the restaurant all the time when her mother wasn't home.

Now Desdemona nibbled on a crispy noo-dle. "So," she said. "We need the perfect revenge for Carlos. You *do* want to get even with him, don't you?"

"I guess so," Sylvie said.

The waiter brought their food. "You've got to show Carlos he can't treat you like this," Desdemona said, squeezing duck sauce on her egg roll.

"That's for sure," Sylvie agreed.

"You have to do something dramatic. Like, show up at his door and give back everything he ever gave you."

"Carlos never gave me very much stuff," Sylvie said. "I never gave him anything, either."

"Then tell McCracken he didn't do any work on the project. That'd serve him right!"

"Carlos did do some of the work," Sylvie pointed out. "Not much, but some."

Desdemona didn't seem to hear her. "We need a plan," she said thoughtfully. "I know! You can drip olive oil all over the inside of his locker. Then his books will get totally greasy, and it will *never* come out. McCracken will give him detentions for the whole year!"

"That's too mean," Sylvie said.

Desdemona frowned as she finished her egg roll. "Carlos has been pretty mean to you," she said. "You've got to do *something*."

"I know," Sylvie said with a sigh. "But I'm not sure this revenge business will work."

"Maybe we can do something else," Desdemona said. "Something that wouldn't last. Hey! We can spray shaving cream all over the inside of Carlos's locker."

Sylvie thought for a minute. Then she giggled. "Okay," she said.

"We'll have to do it during class," Desdemona went on, "when he can't stop us. How about if I ask McCracken for a pass to the bathroom. And while I'm out, I'll blast Carlos's locker!"

"You can't do it alone," Sylvie said, shaking her head. "We both have to get out of class. What if I say I left a book in my locker a little while later?"

"Perfect!" Desdemona said.

Sylvie thought it was pretty brilliant, too. Then she thought of what their teacher might do if she caught them damaging school property. "I sure hope McCracken doesn't catch us," she said, "or we'll both be goners."

"Sometimes you've got to take a risk," Desdemona said. "And this one is worth it!"

The girls quickly finished the rest of their food. Then they paid the bill and walked outside. Sylvie was wearing her old blue raincoat. Desdemona was wearing a dark green cape.

It was still raining lightly. Cars made a whooshing sound as they drove along Grant Avenue.

"So," Desdemona said. "Who else are you friends with now? I mean, besides me."

"No one really," Sylvie admitted.

"I haven't made that many friends either," Desdemona said. "Do you want to be best friends with me?"

Sylvie liked Desdemona a lot, but the girl *was* a little bossy. And something about saying they'd be best friends didn't feel quite right.

She told Desdemona the truth. "I really want to be friends with you. But it's kind of hard for me to think of anyone except Carlos being my best friend."

"Oh," said Desdemona. "Forget it, then."

Sylvie knew she'd hurt Desdemona's feelings. She felt terrible. *Why does everything keep going wrong?* she thought. All she wanted was for things to be the way they were—before Michael Leontes ever showed up in McCracken's class.

It was late Monday morning. Sylvie sat in class and watched the clock. Ms. McCracken stood at the chalkboard, drawing some sort of cocoon. Sylvie put her chin on her hand and studied her teacher's orange hair. She hoped her own red hair would never end up looking like that.

Sylvie knew she should pay attention to the science lesson. But she had other things to think about. Desdemona had just gotten a pass to the bathroom. Sylvie was going to give her a couple of minutes. Then she'd ask to go to her locker.

"Ms. Levine!" Ms. McCracken's voice snapped hard and loud. "Are you paying attention to me or to the clock?"

"To you," Sylvie said.

"Then why don't you tell the class about

the life cycle of the cicada?"

Sylvie didn't know the first thing about a cicada's life cycle. "Uh..." she began. "A cicada is a—a bug. It's born. And then it grows up. And then it dies."

Ms. McCracken raised one orange eyebrow. "Is that all you have to say?"

"Yes," Sylvie said, miserably.

"Ms. Santiago," the teacher said, turning to Rosa. "Would *you* like to tell the class about cicadas?"

"Sure." Rosa stood up quickly. "There are two main types of cicadas," she began. "Right now we're studying the seventeen-year locust. The larvae spend from two to seventeen years in the ground feeding on roots. So the cicadas appear about once every seventeen years."

"Thank you, Ms. Santiago," the teacher said, nodding. "Now, Ms. Levine, were you paying attention to me or to the clock?"

"The clock," Sylvie mumbled.

"See me after school, please," Ms. McCracken said. "And now, class, please take out your workbooks."

Sylvie groaned and put her head down on the desk. She didn't care if McCracken saw her. So far, she had the most detentions in the whole class—even more than Ronnie Smith! Still, she couldn't leave Desdemona out there in the hall on her own.

Sylvie sat up and raised her hand.

"I left my science workbook in my locker," she said when the teacher called on her.

"Very well," Ms. McCracken said. "You may get it—but quickly, please. Next time, be more prepared."

Sylvie ran out of the classroom. Desdemona was waiting by Carlos's locker.

"Do you have the shaving cream?" Sylvie whispered.

"It's in my locker," Desdemona said.

The girls quickly got the can of shaving cream that Sylvie had "borrowed" from her dad. Then they hurried back to Carlos's locker.

Sylvie knew the combination and opened it right up. Then she stood staring into the open locker. Carlos's books for Ms. Rivers's class were on the top shelf. His jacket hung from a hook. In the bottom of the locker was a pair of new sneakers. Carlos's locker was a lot neater than his room at home.

Desdemona wrinkled her nose. "Not very interesting."

"We can put shaving cream all over everything but his books," Sylvie decided.

"He can wash the rest of the things."

"Let's do it!" Desdemona said. She shook the can of shaving cream and handed it to Sylvie. "You first."

Sylvie took a deep breath and pushed the button on the top of the can.

Creamy white foam shot into Carlos's locker. It dripped down the back and ran into the tops of his sneakers.

Desdemona laughed. "Hey, this is fun! Can I do some now?"

"Sure." Sylvie handed her the can and watched in satisfaction as Desdemona sprayed shaving cream all along the sleeve of Carlos's jacket.

"Are you two enjoying yourselves?" asked an angry voice.

Sylvie didn't even have to look up to know who had caught them.

"Ms. DuMonde, may I have that can of shaving cream?"

Without a word, Desdemona handed over the can to Ms. McCracken. The teacher held the can away from her, looking at it with disgust.

"Now you may both get wet towels from the girls' room and clean this mess up," she said. "Then I'll expect you back in the class-room immediately. And I will see both of you in detention every day this week!"

Desdemona looked at Sylvie in shock as the teacher marched away. "She just gave us *five* detentions!"

"That means I have nine all together now," Sylvie muttered. "In the first month of school!"

When lunchtime came, Sylvie had no appetite. She didn't even go to the cafeteria. Instead, she went out to the schoolyard so she could sit somewhere by herself. She didn't want to talk to anyone, not even Desdemona.

Ronnie Smith hadn't gone to the cafeteria either. She was standing in a corner of the schoolyard with her friends. "Yo, Levine!" she called to Sylvie.

Sylvie pretended not to hear her.

"I'm talking to you, wimp," Ronnie said. She came over and stood right in front of Sylvie. Then she gave Sylvie's shoulder a push. "I still owe you—you and your wussy chicken friend with the glasses."

"Carlos is not a chicken," Sylvie said.

"He ran from me," Ronnie reminded her. "He was scared."

"You looked pretty scared yourself that day in the cemetery," Sylvie retorted. "You're the real chicken!"

Ronnie shoved Sylvie hard, and Sylvie landed on the blacktop with a *thud*. Laughing, Ronnie reached down and grabbed Sylvie's pack.

"Hey, give me that!" Sylvie shouted.

Ronnie ignored her. She unzipped the pack and took out Sylvie's blue leather notebook. "I told you I was gonna take this," she said. "Now it's mine."

Sylvie fought back tears of anger. "No one will believe you," she said. "Everyone in the whole class knows that's my notebook."

"So I won't bring it to school," Ronnie said with a shrug. "Maybe I'll give it to my little brother. He'll probably eat it and puke it up."

Ronnie and her gang left the schoolyard, laughing. Sylvie didn't get up right away. Her blue leather notebook was gone. And Ronnie Smith had won again. Why didn't Ms. McCracken ever show up at the right time?

That afternoon Sylvie stayed after school and wrote "I will pay attention in class" one hundred times. Then she wrote "I will not deface school property" one hundred times. By the time she was done, her hand felt as though it was going to fall off.

As she walked out of the building, she half

expected to see Ronnie. Instead, Desdemona was waiting for her.

"Hi," Sylvie said. "How come you're still here?"

Desdemona smiled. "I didn't have to write as many sentences as you did. I figured you could use someone to walk home with."

Sylvie felt better for the first time all afternoon. "Thanks," she said.

"I heard about what happened at lunch," Desdemona said. "Cheryl and Jodi were bragging about the whole thing. Why didn't you tell McCracken that Ronnie took your notebook?"

"Because Ronnie Smith kills people who rat on her," Sylvie said.

"Well, someone's got to stop that girl," Desdemona said.

"Yeah, sure. But it's not going to be me," Sylvie said. "I've got enough problems." She shrugged. "It was just a notebook. I can get another one." But she knew she'd never find another notebook exactly like that.

The girls passed Pat's Tavern and Chang's Chinese Restaurant. Then they went by the stationery store and Luigi's Pizza Parlor.

Desdemona stopped as they reached the Music Corner. "Want to go in?" she asked. "There's a new CD I want to look at."

"I'm already late," Sylvie said.

"Okay," Desdemona said. "I'll go some other time." Suddenly, her eyes widened. "Look out!" she said.

Sylvie jumped back. Michael Leontes and Eric Holland were racing out of the Music Corner.

Quick as a flash, Desdemona stuck out her foot. Michael tripped right over it and fell to the sidewalk. Eric tripped over Michael and landed on top of him. There was a clattering sound as dozens of cassette tapes fell out into the street. More tapes tumbled out of Eric's jacket.

"You guys stole all those tapes!" Sylvie said, shocked.

"They certainly did," said an angry-looking man who had appeared from the store. He reached down and grabbed the two boys' arms. "Let's go," he said. "I'm going to take you no-good shoplifters back inside and call the cops. Then we'll call your parents."

"Ha!" Desdemona said, as the man dragged Michael and Eric away. "That'll show *them.*"

Sylvie nodded. "That was pretty good, Desdemona. I'm just glad Carlos wasn't with them, though."

Desdemona walked Sylvie all the way to

her house. "Looks like you've got a visitor," she said.

Carlos was sitting on Sylvie's front steps. His backpack was beside him. And he had a black eye.

"Hey, Sylvie," Carlos said. "I've been waiting for you."

"I'd better go," Desdemona said quickly.

"No, that's okay," Sylvie said. The last thing she wanted to do right now was talk to Carlos by herself. "Why don't you come upstairs?"

"I can't," Desdemona said, shaking her head.

"Why not?" Sylvie asked.

"Because," Desdemona said, "a good actress always knows when to make her exit."

She waved and walked off. Sylvie stayed on the sidewalk, looking up at Carlos. The two of them had been best friends for more than three years. They used to talk about everything, but now she didn't know what to say. And why did Carlos have that black eye?

Sylvie knew she should talk to Carlos. She was dying to ask him about his eye, too. But seeing him there on her steps made her feel hurt all over again.

I'll just walk right past him, Sylvie decided. She started up the stairs.

"Sylvie, wait," Carlos said. "I heard what happened with Ronnie. Thanks for sticking up for me."

"I shouldn't have," Sylvie said coldly.

"You're still mad, aren't you?" Carlos chipped a piece of paint off the railing. "Newton misses you, you know."

Sylvie put her key in the door. "See you later, Carlos," she said.

"Sylvie," Carlos said. "I want to talk to you."

"Well, I don't want to talk to *you!*" Sylvie said.

"Neither do Christina and Roberto," Carlos said. He put his head in his hands. "Everyone hates me now."

Sylvie reached for the doorknob.

"Look, I'm sorry," Carlos called. "I never should have been so mean to you. I should have worked more on our project. And I shouldn't have acted like Michael was more important than you." He looked down at the stairs. "I should have acted more like a friend."

"Did you know that your buddy Michael steals things?" Sylvie asked. "He and Eric took a whole bunch of tapes from the Music Corner today. And they got caught."

Carlos gave a low whistle. "Michael said he and Eric were going to lift some stuff. He wanted me to go with them."

"So why didn't you?" Sylvie asked.

Carlos looked up at her angrily. "Why do you think?"

Sylvie went over and sat down on the step beside him. "Because you're not a thief."

"I'm not going to hang with Michael anymore. He's not as cool as I thought he was."

Sylvie was quiet for a minute. "And now you want to hang out with me again?"

"That's not how it is," Carlos said slowly. "It's not like I ever stopped wanting to hang

114

out with you. But sometimes I need to be with other people, too. Like the guys."

"So you can play football?"

Carlos looked away. "Not really. But there's just some stuff I can do with guys that I can't do with a girl. Besides, you're friends with that new girl now, aren't you? Desdemona what's-her-name?"

"DuMonde," Sylvie told him. "So?"

"So aren't there some things you can do with her that you can't do with me?"

Sylvie thought about that. She never could have danced with Carlos, or dressed up, or put on makeup. And Desdemona had been a really good friend so far. "I guess," she admitted.

"But that doesn't mean you and I have to stop being friends," Carlos pointed out.

Sylvie smiled at Carlos. "You're right. Maybe we just have to hang out with other people, too."

"So," Carlos said, "can we work on the model together again?"

Sylvie hesitated. They only had four days left. She knew how to make the planes now, but she could definitely use help. "Okay," she said.

Carlos stuck out his hand. "Partners?"

"Partners," Sylvie agreed. She and Carlos

shook on it. "But what about Newton?" Sylvie asked. "Roberto told me your landlord said he had to be out in a week."

"By next Saturday," Carlos said glumly. "I don't want to give the little guy up, but I know we have to. Maybe we should take him to Harry Park and make a sign. That way, maybe someone will *see* how cute he is and adopt him right there."

"We can try," Sylvie said with a sigh.

Carlos stood up. "Let's go work on our project."

Sylvie nodded, and they started up the stairs together.

"Oh, wait a minute," Carlos said, as Sylvie opened the door. "There's something I forgot to give you." He reached into his pack and took out her blue leather notebook.

Sylvie couldn't believe it. She took the notebook and hugged it to her chest. "Where did you get this?"

Carlos looked away.

Sylvie's eyes widened. "Is *that* how you got the black eye?"

Carlos shrugged. "Ronnie's not that tough. Don't forget, Roberto's been beating up on me for years."

Sylvie just stared at him for a minute. Carlos had fought Ronnie for *her!* "Thanks,

Carlos," she said. And then she gave him a big smile.

For the rest of the week, as soon as Sylvie got out of detention, Sylvie and Carlos worked on their project. Sylvie finished all the windows in the terminal and made a landing strip out of black construction paper. Carlos made four model airplanes and a baggage cart with tiny suitcases on it. Together they painted the terminal and put blue Christmas lights on the landing strip.

Sylvie visited the kitten every morning before school. She didn't know what would happen if they couldn't find someone to adopt him. All she knew was that after Saturday, Newton couldn't go back to the Ortegas'.

On Friday morning, the day the class projects were due, Sylvie and Carlos brought their model to school. Sylvie looked around the classroom. Kareem Jackson's desk was pushed next to Sharon Fuller's. The two desktops were covered with the striped cliffs of the Grand Canyon. Eric Holland had a little Shea Stadium on his desk. Annie Tuzmarti had her model covered with a pillowcase. Ronnie Smith had something on her desk that looked like a giant cigar. Sylvie remembered that Ronnie and her partner,

Cheryl, were doing a model of the submarine on exhibit at the Parkside Museum.

Ms. McCracken entered the room and smiled as she saw all the projects. "These look very promising," she told the class. "I can see that you've all worked hard. Who wants to show their model first?"

Sylvie looked at Carlos. "Rosa," he whispered.

Sure enough, Rosa Santiago waved her hand. Ms. McCracken asked Rosa and John Jerome to bring their project to the front of the room.

Sylvie couldn't believe it. The real thing was even better than the photographs. Rosa and John had made the Lincoln and Jefferson memorials, the Washington Monument, and the Vietnam Wall. The Vietnam Wall was made out of cardboard and covered with shiny black mirrors. Sylvie could see that Rosa had neatly painted tiny names on it.

Rosa talked about the memorials and when they were built. She talked the most about the Vietnam Wall, and how it was covered with the names of all the soldiers who'd died in the Vietnam War. John didn't say a lot. Sylvie had the feeling again that he hadn't done much of the work himself.

"And why did you choose this project?" Ms.

McCracken asked when they were done.

Rosa looked down at the floor. "My uncle's name is on the wall," she answered. "I sort of did this for him."

Sylvie decided that Rosa wasn't a total alien, after all. She felt really sorry that Rosa's uncle had died.

Next Michael and Eric talked about Shea Stadium. Sylvie thought that was pretty boring. She wondered what had happened after the man at the music store had called the police. The boys didn't seem that upset.

Desdemona talked about the Delacorte Theater, and how great it was to have a place in the city where everyone could see free plays. Then she did a short scene from one of the plays she'd seen there. Everyone in the class clapped—even Ms. McCracken.

Annie Tuzmarti and Sasha Sommers unveiled their model of Harry Park. There was a building Sylvie had never seen on the duck pond. And the duck pond looked a lot bigger.

"The duck pond used to be a lake," Annie explained. "And this building here was a boat house. Harry Park used to have rowboats and canoes. But there was a lot of rain in 1925, and the lake flooded. So they filled most of it in and turned it into a pond."

119

"Oh, man!" David Jaffe said. "They used to have boats. All we get is ducks!"

"Mr. Jaffe, you know better than to talk out of turn," Ms. McCracken said. "See me after school, please."

Sylvie and Carlos were up next. Sylvie felt very nervous as they carried their model over to an electrical socket. They had never really figured out what they were going to say. Luckily, Carlos knew all sorts of facts about Kennedy Airport from his father. He told the class about all the traffic that the airport handled. He also talked about what went on in an airplane terminal—especially the things passengers never see. Then Sylvie plugged in the model to the wall socket and all the lights went on. She showed the planes making night landings and taking off. Everyone seemed to think that was pretty exciting.

"Very good," said Ms. McCracken when they'd finished. "For a while there, I wasn't sure you two were going to be able to pull it together."

Neither were we, Sylvie thought. She looked at Carlos and grinned. He gave her a thumbs-up and grinned back.

16

It was Saturday morning. Sylvie was baby-sitting Willa again. Her little sister was watching cartoons, but Sylvie wasn't really paying attention. Today she and Carlos had to give Newton away. What if they couldn't find a home for him?

The doorbell rang.

"Roberto!" Willa said, clapping her hands. "He's nice. I'm going to marry him," she told Sylvie.

"It's not Roberto," Sylvie told her. "Roberto doesn't visit three-year-olds." She went to the intercom and pressed the button.

"It is I!" someone said.

Sylvie giggled. "Come on up, Desdemona," she said.

When Desdemona arrived in the doorway, her eyes widened with delight. "This is so great!" she said.

"What is?" Sylvie asked, looking around.

"The apartment! And everything in it! I mean, look at this lamp!"

Sylvie gazed back at the lamp. Now that her favorite couch was gone, the lamp stood out more. Its shade was made of stained glass, in ugly orange and beige. Sylvie had always hated that lamp.

"And check out the mirror!" Desdemona said. She stood in front of the oval wooden mirror and struck a pose. "I love it!"

"Really?" Sylvie said doubtfully.

Desdemona plopped down on the new flowered couch Mrs. Levine had brought home and put her arm over her forehead. "This would be great for a tragic love scene," she said. Then she sat up. "Your apartment is filled with great props, Sylvie. It's not like all that boring modern stuff we have. We could even do plays here!"

"I want to be the star!" Willa said. "I'm a good star."

"You're a pest," Sylvie told her.

Mr. and Mrs. Levine came out of the kitchen. "Well, and who have we here?" Sylvie's father asked, looking at Desdemona.

Desdemona gave him a big smile. "I'm Desdemona DuMonde," she said.

Mr. Levine gave a little bow. "I'm honored

to finally meet you in person, Ms. DuMonde."

"Welcome, Desdemona," Mrs. Levine said. "Are you going to go to the park with Sylvie and Carlos this afternoon?"

Desdemona nodded.

"I want to go, too," Willa said, jumping up and down.

"I'll take her, Mom," Sylvie offered. "She's never seen Newton. It's her last chance."

"I'll tell you what," Mrs. Levine said to Willa. "Joyce is coming over now to baby-sit. I'll have her take you to the park so you can see the kitten."

"Okay," Willa said, pouting a little.

A few minutes later, Sylvie and Desdemona arrived at Carlos's house.

"Desdemona's going to help us find a family for Newton," Sylvie said.

"Okay," Carlos said. "I've got him all ready to go. He's in my room."

Sylvie and Desdemona followed Carlos down the hall. Sylvie couldn't believe what she was seeing. The whole Ortega family was in Carlos's room, petting Newton. The kitten was wearing a little red collar.

"This is Desdemona, everyone," Sylvie said. "Desdemona, that's Newton."

Christina picked up the purring kitten. "We're going to miss you," she said.

Roberto tweaked the kitten's ear. "Yeah," he said. "I'd rather share my room with you than with Carlos."

Carlos punched Roberto in the ribs.

Christina handed Newton to Sylvie. "Carlos has a leash for him. And Roberto made a box that you can carry him in."

Newton touched Sylvie's neck with his cold little nose. Sylvie hugged him closer and blinked back tears. She spoke very softly so only Newton could hear. "I'll miss you more than anyone," she told him. "You'll always be my cat."

"Come on, Sylvie," Carlos said. "Let's go." He had one of Christina's flyers in his hand.

All the Ortegas saw them to the door and waved good-bye.

Sylvie, Carlos, and Desdemona didn't talk much as they set off for Harry Park. Carlos carried the box with Newton inside. Sylvie carried the leash and some extra cat food. Desdemona carried the sign.

It was a warm fall day. The sky was bright blue. On Grant Avenue the trees were turning gold and red.

Newton the store owner was sitting on a folding chair in front of his newsstand. "Hey

there, kids," he called. "Why are you all looking so down today?"

"Hi, Newton," Sylvie said. She pointed to
the mewing box that Carlos held. "Remember
our kitten?"

"That fine little gray-and-white cat?"

Carlos nodded. "We have to give him away
today. My landlord won't let us keep him."

Newton eyed Desdemona. "And who is
this?"

"This is Desdemona DuMonde," Sylvie
said. "She's a new friend of ours. Desdemona,
this is Newton."

Desdemona looked confused. "But that's
your cat's name."

"We named the cat after Newton," Sylvie
explained. "Because the day we found little
Newton, big Newton helped us out."

"You named him after me?" Newton said.
"And you never told me? Let me see this little
cat who's walking around with my name."

Carlos put the box on the ground and took
the kitten out. "Here," he said, handing the
cat to Newton.

The store owner lifted the kitten onto his
lap. The kitten immediately began to purr.

"You know, kids," Newton said a few
moments later. "I have a big problem. Maybe

you can help me out. I've had some nasty mice in the store at night. I've been catching them with the kind of traps that don't hurt them. And I've been setting them free in the park. But I think they just come right back."

A slow grin spread over Carlos's face. "I think you need a cat!"

"Maybe I do," Newton agreed. "Mice don't come around if they smell a cat."

"You mean you'll adopt him?" Sylvie asked.

"Well, I couldn't take him home with me," Newton said. "He'd live here in the store. But he'd be mighty happy, I bet."

"Could we visit him?" Sylvie asked.

"Anytime you want." Newton winked at them. "There's just one thing."

"What?" Carlos asked.

"Two Newtons in one place is too confusing." The store owner lifted up the little cat and looked him in the eye. "From now on, you're Junior. All right?"

Junior purred.

"That's much better," Desdemona said. "I was getting confused, too."

Sylvie held out the extra cat food. "We can offer you a starter kit."

"I'll take it," Newton said. Then he put Junior in her arms. "Why don't you carry him into the store? We'll see about making him a nice cozy bed."

Sylvie called home from Newton's store. She told Joyce that Willa should come to the newsstand if she wanted to see the kitten. Then Carlos called his family and told them the news, too.

Newton frowned. "There's not enough room in this store for all the people who are going to visit this cat."

"He'll bring you more business," Carlos

Newton laughed. "All right!"

Carlos turned to Sylvie and Desdemona. "So now what do you want to do?"

"We could go to the park anyway," Desdemona said. "Maybe there's a soccer game going on."

"You play soccer?" Sylvie asked in surprise.

"Sure," Desdemona said with a shrug. "I never mentioned that?"

As the three of them set off for Harry Park, Sylvie couldn't remember feeling happier. Maybe she didn't have a real best friend anymore. But she had two very good friends. And a great little cat.

Don't miss the next book in the
McCracken's Class series:

McCracken's Class #2:
ANNIE'S RAINBOW

Annie gulped hard. Ronnie wouldn't destroy her here in the cafeteria, would she?

"Uh...hi, Ronnie," Annie said. "What's happening?"

"Actually, I thought you might know nie said. "Somebody attacked me in the this morning with those sticky things the trees. It was a girl. I saw her."

"You...um...did?" said Annie.

"Not real well, but she looked a lot like you." Ronnie leaned closer. "Listen, you're a cool kid. You hear stuff. If you find out who did it, I want you to tell me right away. Got it?"

"Sure, Ronnie," Annie said.

Ronnie pounded her on the shoulder. "I know I can count on you."

"Sure," Annie repeated. "Absolutely."

But as Ronnie walked away, Annie started to feel dizzy. Now some unsuspecting, uncool kid was going to be dead meat—because of what she, Annie Tuzmarti, had done!